The Negotiator

By HelenKay Dimon

The Negotiator

A GAMES PEOPLE PLAY
CHRISTMAS NOVELLA

HELENKAY DIMON

AVONIMPULSE
An Imprint of HarperCollinsPublishers

HarperCollins
PUBLISHERS
— Since 1817 —

Excerpt from *The Pretender* copyright © 2018 by HelenKay Dimon.

THE NEGOTIATOR. Copyright © 2017 by HelenKay Dimon. All rights reserved. Printed in the United States of America. No part of this book may be used or reproduced in any manner whatsoever without written permission except in the case of brief quotations embodied in critical articles and reviews. For information, address HarperCollins Publishers, 195 Broadway, New York, NY 10007.

Digital Edition NOVEMBER 2017 ISBN: 978-0-06-274984-0
Print Edition ISBN: 978-0-06-274985-7

Cover photograph by Yasmeen Anderson Photography

Avon Impulse and the Avon Impulse logo are registered trademarks of HarperCollins Publishers in the United States of America.

Avon and HarperCollins are registered trademarks of HarperCollins Publishers in the United States of America and other countries.

FIRST EDITION

17 18 19 20 21 OPM 10 9 8 7 6 5 4 3 2 1

This one is for all the awesome fans who asked for Garrett's story. I love him, too. Here he is . . .

The Negotiator

Chapter One

He rose from the dead.

Lauren Gallagher couldn't come up with any other explanation. Her once-dead husband was very much alive and standing on the other side of her front door . . . and she felt nothing but numbness spreading inside her.

For a man who supposedly washed overboard in the middle of a violent storm, he looked pretty healthy. Big smile. Bright white teeth. Khaki pants and deck shoes. She'd forgotten how much she hated the deck shoes.

The wattage on his super smile dimmed a bit as he shifted his weight from foot to foot and rubbed his hands up and down his arms. "Aren't you going to let me in?"

Her mind went blank. The world flipped sideways on her and her stomach rolled. The whole time she could hear him talking but the words didn't make sense. None of this made sense. She opened her mouth but nothing came out but a tiny gasping sound. That's all she could muster as she blinked, trying to process what she was seeing.

"Lauren? Why are you just standing there? Open this door."

An order. The sharp smack in his voice sounded far too familiar. That quickly it brought her crashing back to reality.

She really wanted to say no to his command. Not that she hadn't mourned him. Even with the dysfunctional state of their faltering marriage at the time he disappeared, she had. She'd grieved for what could have been and the dreams that fizzled out early in their time together. She grieved for his loss as she would an old friend, not as a person she viewed as her soulmate, if there even was such a thing.

That was less than three years ago. The police had arrived and she'd dropped to her knees feeling sick and hollow at the idea of Carl gasping for breath as the water he loved so much overtook him.

Months had passed slowly after that. She'd been locked in a perpetual state of shock, topped off with a wallop of guilt because she'd visited a divorce attorney for the first time just before he disappeared. With him gone she'd found out about the lies. His hidden debts and how he'd taken their business to the brink of bankruptcy, all while showing her fake bank statements he'd manufactured. He'd gone to a lot of trouble to carry on the ruse of pretending their finances were fine.

And then things had gotten even worse. All those whispers about Maryanne, the girlfriend who seemed to be an open secret to everyone except Lauren. The one who, unlike Lauren, did not have any debts or an unpaid mortgage or a business on the verge of bankruptcy. Maryanne Lightwood, the same woman who'd mysteriously walked out on her rent and left town right as Carl's boat disappeared.

Lauren prided herself on being practical. She was skeptical of coincidences and not stupid, so confusion had turned to fury in record time. As the cool December wind blew in the front door of the small cottage now, she realized the fury still simmered inside her.

She lived far enough from the water that the breeze wasn't frigid, but it carried a bite. For the past few years early winter in Annapolis, Maryland, had meant an unwelcome amount of snow. This year had been mild. As someone who ran a pleasure boat and fishing tour business and depended on tourists, she thought she might get lucky this year and only have to survive a short off-season.

Apparently, her luck had just run out.

"Lauren, honey?" Carl pulled on the handle of the screen door. When it didn't immediately open, he shook it, rattling it in the door frame. Still, it didn't move.

She'd never been so grateful for her lock-the-door paranoia. He should be happy, too, because the thin screen might be all that was saving his sorry lying ass right now.

Under the numbness and shock lurked a layer of bubbling resentment and rage. She'd kept up the outward farce of being fine for so long that she'd started to believe it. Now the mask slipped. She wanted to throw open the door and pound on his chest and make him apologize for every wrong.

But Carl had never taken responsibility for anything in his life. Even now he had the nerve to stand there with a stupid look on his stupid face, as if she were the unreasonable one for not welcoming him home with a big hug. So, yeah, the door stayed closed for his protection because she knew once she unleashed her temper she would not stop.

"Hey, what is this?" Carl's hand dropped to his side as he frowned at her through the mesh screen. "Honey, I'm back."

Honey? What kind of man checked out of his life for almost three years and expected to step right back into it, no questions asked? It was as if he were empty inside, without a conscience. And he was so close to getting a kick in his junk.

"Yeah, I can see that." She tried to swallow but couldn't choke down the lump of anger racing up her throat. "Tell me, where have you've been?"

"Lauren, Jesus. It's freezing out here. Let me in." He pulled on the handle again as if he expected a different result than last time. The door made a thumping sound as it hit the frame. "What's wrong with you? Snap out of it."

He kept up that tone. Short, dismissive, demanding. The only time he hadn't been obnoxious was during the years when she thought he was dead. Even then . . .

That's all it took. Something inside her snapped and wave after wave of uncontrolled, boiling-hot rage raced through her. He wasn't the only one who could throw his attitude and his I'm-done tone around. "Where the hell have you been, Carl? You don't contact me at all and then you just stroll up to my door. You ripped my life, my work—my everything—apart and now act as if you've only been gone for an afternoon. What is wrong with you? What happened?"

"I was left for dead." His surfer-boy good looks faded a bit as his eyes narrowed. "Thanks in part to you." Wherever he'd been he must have forgotten how locks worked because he rattled the door one more time. "Now open this."

He was blaming her. *Of course he was.* She was likely at fault for the fact his hair wasn't the same sunny blond it once was and for the few wrinkles at the corners of his eyes. He was forty-one, having celebrated two birthdays while he was gone. She doubted he was taking the transition out of his thirties all that well.

She'd been thirty-three and inching very close to thirty-four when he went missing and even back then he'd mentioned "hip spread" more than once. Hers, of course. Not his. She'd expected him to battle aging as fiercely as he'd fought to be the only one in charge of handling the bills. Now she knew why . . . because he hadn't bothered to actually pay any debt with her name on it.

"You disappeared." Right there, in that moment, she kind of wished he'd do it again and had to push back the wave of guilt that came with that realization. She'd had no idea how much hate had festered inside her until he popped up again. The frowning, his ridiculous summer shoes in winter, that voice—it all worked on her nerves and it had been less than ten minutes.

"A wave hit the boat. It tipped and I went overboard." He shrugged. "Are you satisfied now?"

Not even close. A hundred questions filled her head. "Who could be satisfied with that? What's the rest of the story?"

His body language and easy dismissal of how his terrible choices impacted her life only made her more determined to understand what his days looked like during the last few years. Then maybe she'd let him in, but probably not.

He waved her off. "None of that matters now."

"It does to me." His short nonanswers ticked her off even more, and she wouldn't have said that was possible. "I deserve an explanation. A real one. All of the facts, not just pieces."

He leaned in closer as his jaw tightened. "I said later."

Wariness surged through her. She wasn't afraid. No, *scared* wasn't the right word. Carl had never been violent, never raised a hand or threatened her. But near the end he'd been distant and that had turned into flashes of meanness. Snide comments about how he'd married a woman but got stuck with a fisherman. Sudden outbursts of blaming her for the fact that they weren't making more money in the boating business.

So much confusion swirled around him and his stories and all that deception. She'd convinced herself he ran off with his girlfriend. Not that she ever admitted that to anyone or said the words out loud. No, there had been too much at risk.

To save her house and business she'd needed the life insurance and a final judgment from the court about Carl's fate. A confirmation that he was legally dead. She had to pretend to believe it. It had taken her almost two years to persuade the court and wrestle the business and house away from the legal no-man's-land it had wound up in when he disappeared. The life insurance company had refused to pay on the claim. That meant she'd had to salvage what she could with him gone.

Now he was back, and as much as she hated it, they needed to talk. She tried, even as her brain screamed for her to slam the door. "I think we should—"

"I can't believe you're being a pain in the ass."

Her head snapped back at the fury lacing his voice. "Me?"

"Jake warned me you'd gone from grieving to stone cold in a matter of months." Carl shook his head. "I didn't believe it. Not after everything we'd been through."

She lost the thread of the conversation as soon as Carl mentioned his brother. "Jake?"

"That's where I'll be. At his house." Carl started to shift away from the door. "But get your act together and do it fast, Lauren. I plan on being in this house and back at work by Christmas."

"That's two weeks away."

"I'll be back tomorrow." He made a face that suggested he was sick of her again already. "Be over your shock and ready to talk by then."

Lauren watched Carl walk back down the path to the car parked on the street. She recognized the dark sedan. It belonged to Carl's brother, which meant Carl had gone there first.

Her mind spun with questions about where he'd been and why he was back. She had no idea how he planned to explain and argue his way out of this . . . or why he thought he could walk back into her life now without any real explanation or sign of remorse.

A gust of cold air got her moving. She slammed the front door closed and rested her palm on it. Tried to breathe in, to think.

Her usual calm detachment abandoned her. Jumbled thoughts crashed into her brain. Panic rose in her chest, threatening to swamp her. Finding a lost husband should be a good thing. For her, it amounted to a nightmare. Everything was upside down and all she wanted was to right it again.

Help. She never asked anyone for help. Not ever. She'd learned long ago that needing someone, depending on them, led to heartache and disappointment. But

Garrett McGrath's face kept flashing in her mind. Sarcastic, charming, sinfully handsome Garrett. They'd met in the summer and he'd asked her out for two months. Hanging around, texting, insisting he'd wait for her to be ready to date again.

The guy had honed his tall-dark-and-smoldering look and for some reason he'd decided to aim it full force at her. Probably had something to do with the thrill of the chase. That was the only answer she could come up with. Because once he knew her, really knew her, he'd back off. Any sane person would.

But right now, as the walls closed in and she struggled to hold on to a coherent thought, all she could do was think of his face. The dark brown hair and those big green eyes. That firm chin . . . and his uncanny ability to solve complex problems while making a joke and without breaking a sweat.

She glanced around her cottage. It had a beachy vibe with weathered white beadboard walls and overstuffed blue furniture. It consisted of two small bedrooms, a bathroom and a joint living and eating area. Her refuge. The place she'd rented when she lost everything else. The same place Carl for some reason thought he had a right to live in.

She grabbed her cell off the couch and dialed the number Garrett had put in there when they first met. The phone rang and his deep voice came on the line. Voice mail.

She waited a few moments. Gave herself a bit of a

pep talk and mentally insisted she could handle this, just like she handled everything else.

Instead of leaving a message she texted him. She tried to think of the right thing to say. She went with the only words that made sense to her . . . You were right. Carl is not dead.

GARRETT STARED AT the text message. It had come in a half hour ago. He'd missed it while he was parking his car in the airport lot. His flight to San Francisco left in an hour. He would have enough time to maneuver his way through security, grab a coffee and get to the gate, and even that was pushing it. Now this.

He'd been trying to win Lauren's trust for months. With Christmas coming and her refusing to commit to seeing him, Garrett had booked a last-minute flight to visit with the only family he had left. His aunt and cousin, Lotti. The goal was to see his aunt before she left on a cruise then annoy Lotti for a few days before taking off on his own. That was about all the family time he could muster for *this* holiday.

His parents had died in a car crash exactly one month after he turned nineteen. Christmas Eve almost twelve years ago. He'd been in college and orphaned in a matter of minutes. Too much alcohol had accompanied what many suspected was a fight that had started at his dad's work party and continued into the car . . . and then they were gone.

The devastation had lingered for so much longer than Garrett had expected. He was an adult when it happened, or almost. He knew he'd grieve but he'd thought that would end and then he'd move on. Being alone wouldn't matter because he wasn't a kid. He would be fine. But his aunt had known better and explained that type of mourning was a forever process. She'd wrapped him in a blanket of love and given him an extended family, and his cousin had become the little sister he never had.

They were expecting him. He'd promised to come out for a week before the holidays and maybe again after. They didn't want him to be alone on the anniversary of his parents' death, but he'd long ago learned that he operated better on his own that day. Quiet and still, wondering what could have been if his father had just called a cab.

For once December had rolled around and he wasn't thinking only of his parents. He hadn't buried himself in work to battle back the memories. That had been the plan, but now he had Lauren's text.

You were right. Carl is not dead.

The clipped sentences fit Lauren. She wasn't the flowery type. She was practical and beautiful and smart. She never volunteered information, except to insist their more than five-year age difference mattered. When he refused to accept that as an excuse for not going out with him because it was ridiculous, she informed him that she was a mess and that he could do better.

If she'd said she wasn't interested, he would have

walked away disappointed, but he would have gone. Not having dinner because of some perceived failing she had about herself? That part he couldn't agree to.

For the first time since he'd met Lauren, she needed him. He hated the idea of her being targeted by a con man ex, but he loved that he was the one she had on speed dial for anything.

Yeah, his family trip could wait. They'd understand because that's what they did. They were bone-deep decent. They gave him room and reeled him in now and then when he failed to call often enough. Lotti would give him shit for picking a woman over them, so he decided to keep that information quiet for now. He'd call this a work problem. He could almost see Lotti rolling her eyes at that one.

He dialed his aunt as he turned around and headed back to his car. A shot of anxiety surged through him, making him speed up the pace with each step. He had the sudden need to race to Annapolis.

Carl Gallagher's being alive made Garrett want to kill him.

Chapter Two

HOURS LATER GARRETT walked next to Lauren on their way back to her house after picking up takeout Thai food from a place a few streets away. To him delivery had sounded sensible but he lost that battle when she'd insisted on getting out for a few minutes. He now knew that was code for *walking until Garrett's balls freeze*.

He'd been in town for about an hour and they still hadn't talked about *it*. Carl stepping back into her life understandably threw her off, made her more quiet than usual. Since arriving Garrett had gotten little more than a steady drumbeat of silence from her.

She wasn't ready to talk. Fine, he got that. Having a not-so-dead husband spring up, making demands, had to be a shock. Garrett wasn't handling the news that much better. The killing rage inside him had subsided but the idea of punching Carl in the face still sounded good. He'd already called Wren and put him on this Carl guy's trail.

If Carl thought he was just going to pop up and re-kindle his stalled marriage . . . Jesus, Garrett didn't even want to think about that. His relationship, or whatever it was, with Lauren had barely moved past "Go" but damn if he didn't want to fast-forward them to something beyond friends who saw each other once or twice a week and texted every day.

Hell, he dreamed about her. Thought about her out on that boat and working on the marina and it was all he could do not to bolt from his office an hour away and come see her. A strange unseen string connected them. He didn't get it, couldn't explain it, but he'd experienced her fierce loyalty and stark determination up close and he wanted to see more.

The biting December wind nipped at his skin through his black driving gloves as they walked. His boots thud-ded on the pavement as the heavy scent of burning fire-wood hung in the air. He'd bet every house on the street put their fireplace to use tonight.

It was after eight and dark clouds filled the sky. He figured there would never be a better time to launch into an unwanted conversation, so he took the plunge. "What did Carl say when he came to the house?"

She sighed as she tucked her hands into her jacket pockets. "Nothing."

They were one question into this topic and already it was sputtering out. "I'm betting that's not true."

Her focus stayed on the sidewalk in front of her. "We didn't talk about anything."

Garrett bit back his annoyance as he stopped. The move forced her to face him, which was exactly what he wanted. "You're saying that your not-so-dead husband showed up alive and well and talking and shit, and then—what?—just stared at you?"

"Of course not." She bit her bottom lip as her glance grazed his chin then wandered off into the distance behind him. "And technically, he's not my husband."

Yeah, he had some bad news for her on that. "We'll come back to your marital status in a second."

She made a hissing sound. "Lucky me."

Pain echoed in her voice. She rocked back on the heels of her sturdy work boots but didn't bolt as he expected. He knew from his frequent visits to see her and their time out on her boat and the hours spent at the diner dive by her office drinking coffee that she didn't exactly do well with confrontation. He had known her for more than six months, had asked her out on a real date about three months ago and had settled for spending time with her pretending not to date ever since.

She was practical and driven and so hot she made his brain shut down. The combination of the shoulder-length blond hair she generally wore pulled back in a ponytail and those big brown watchful eyes burned through his usual defenses. Sleek, sexy muscles earned from hours of hard work on the boat had his mind spinning with how good she would feel—taste—if he ever got her naked. Even now, deep into cooler weather, her smooth skin carried a hint of a tan and he ached to see the tan lines under her clothes.

Growing up he might have called her a tomboy. He was a dumbass back then. Self-involved and caught up in sports and being popular and shit that stopped mattering to him more than a decade ago. He had just turned thirty-one and was smarter now, or so he liked to think.

He looked at her and saw this ass-kicking mix of athletic, powerful and so fucking feminine. She had it all. Stunning face. Full lips. Eyes that telegraphed intelligence and experience and a sort of hard earned wariness. Smoking hot body. Killer legs. He was in for all of it.

He appreciated women who knew what they wanted and fought for it. He was fine with messy and difficult. The idea of dating someone who agreed with everything he said or hung on his every word bored him. Other guys liked that and good for them. He craved a challenge. From the first time he met her, he wanted to learn more about what shaped who she was and how she thought about things. And touch her. Sweet hell, he really wanted to touch her. But not tonight. Maybe not soon thanks to her idiot husband and his piss-poor timing.

"Walk me through his visit. The guy comes to your door and . . . ?" Garrett started walking again. She kept step with his long strides but she didn't say a thing. "The dramatic pause is your cue to talk, by the way. What happened next, Lauren?"

"He wanted in the house. He talked about coming back to work." She made a noise that sounded like a frustrated groan. "Basically, he talked to me like a demanding, jerky boss would talk to one of his employees."

Garrett's hand tightened on the handle of the takeout bag. "So he's still an asshole."

She glanced over at him and smiled. "I never told you he was an asshole."

As if Garrett needed to be walked through that definition. "He pretended to be dead and screwed you both financially and emotionally. The asshole part is implied."

"You're not wrong."

He could hear the smile in her voice. It was the first glimpse of lightness since they'd exchanged texts hours ago. "In the past five minutes you've talked more about him and said more negative things than in the entire six months I've known you."

They'd met when he was in town on an assignment connected to her best friend, Kayla. She had been the one to mention Lauren's "missing" husband. Garrett had tiptoed around the subject of Carl ever since because Lauren had insisted right up until her surprise he's-alive text that Carl was dead. The reality was people generally didn't disappear at sea and Carl was more experienced than most, which made it even less likely for him.

Garrett knew how fraud worked. He worked for a

company that collected information and solved problems. He was second in command to the man people called when they needed confidential assistance. Washington, D.C.'s elusive and mysterious fixer, Levi Wren, known to only a few and even then known only as Wren. The position provided Garrett with a front row to investigation intel, and he knew that as far as ways to die went, disappearing into the sea was a suspect one. But when it came to leaving your spouse and running out on a lot of debt, it seemed to be many people's bizarrely ineffective go-to plan.

They turned the corner and started down her street. They were only a few houses away, which was good because grayish-white puffy clouds filled the sky and the air hinted at incoming snow. His feet were frozen. He'd been packed for a trip to California and not really thinking about facing this weather.

She pulled her keychain out of her pocket and bounced it in her palm. The sound of clanking metal served as background noise. "I was being—"

"Lying."

Her head shot to the side and she stared at him. "What?"

"You were lying." When she frowned, he decided to try a little tact even though every cell inside him yelled for him to push her to get through this story. "Fine. We'll use the word *pretending*. You were *pretending* Carl died in a freak, horrible accident."

"As far as I knew, he had."

Garrett whistled. "Wow."

"What?"

"Your denial. Did you take a class in that? Because damn, woman."

She shook her head as she opened the latch on the small gate leading to the pathway to her front door. "I forgot how difficult you can be."

Garrett didn't follow. He stopped, watching those legs and that fine ass and wondering if she realized how hard she was running from the truth.

"You know, you're allowed to be angry with him. To think he's a piece of shit. That doesn't make you a bad person." Garrett had a feeling he could spend the rest of the week saying those simple words and she'd never believe him. Her blank look suggested her denial was pretty deeply entrenched. "Or you can just stare at me." Which she did. Stared and didn't say a word. "Fine, we'll *pretend* his being alive is a surprise, and we'll ignore the fact you don't seem even a little happy about having a husband again."

Yeah, that last part was a bit of a shot, but it was true. She'd found out her long-lost husband was back just a few hours ago and instead of reconnecting with him she'd texted Garrett. His ego exploded at the thought, but her decision carried a message. He wasn't sure why she couldn't see it or wouldn't admit it.

"I'm not married to him anymore."

Okay, not the response he'd expected. Garrett had expected a fight on a different topic. "Because you had him declared dead? I'm not up on family law but I think having him declared dead is not the same as being divorced."

Her mouth dropped open and stayed there for a second. Then the uncharacteristic stammering and fidgeting started. "I can't . . . No. There's no way . . ."

Even in the dim beam from the porch light Garrett could see all the color drain from her face. Her body seemed to list to one side for a second. He felt sick for her but he also felt some relief.

He nodded. "There you go."

"What?"

"A show of emotion. It's about time." He half wished she would yell. Not at him. No, they could find a better target, like Carl.

Her head shot back and for a second she didn't say anything. "Are you afraid I'm dead inside?"

That was too far. She was closed off and careful, and he was determined to break through to her. "I never said that."

"Oh, really?" She snorted. "You've repeatedly asked me out and I've said no. You don't think maybe I'm all out of energy for emotions and feelings and whatever it is we've been doing that we're not calling dating."

At least they could both admit the whole not-dating thing was getting old, especially when they really kind of were but without the side benefits of kissing, touching and generally getting all over each other. He'd never worked this hard to get close to a woman. He'd even had to convince her to let him clean her boat just to spend a Saturday with her one time. What the fuck was that about?

The whole relationship, friendship, want-to-get-you-naked thing they had going on was a constant source of confusion. He didn't pine. If a woman wasn't interested, he respected that and moved on. Problem was, Lauren made it clear she was interested but the no-trespassing sign still stayed up to keep him at a distance.

For anyone else, he would have given up and walked away. But there was something about her. The joy that thrummed off her when she was on the water or telling work stories. The stark loneliness he sometimes saw in those eyes as she stared off into the distance. He understood the constantly shifting emotions. They boiled and churned inside him as well.

She was complex, interesting and sexy as hell. She had him spinning in circles and rearranging his life just to drive from Washington, DC, to Annapolis once or twice a week to spend time with her.

Really, what the fuck was that about?

If his friends only knew . . . but they didn't. Or they hadn't before Carl showed up again. But his friends were smart and nosy as hell, so they'd figure it out and poke around in his private life. Just one more reason for him to despise Carl.

"I hoped you were playing hard to get." He had to hold on to that theory or he'd completely lose his ability to be rational.

Her blank expression broke into a sunny smile. "Because you're so irresistible."

Her expressions actually rumbled inside him. He could *feel* her smile in his gut and he didn't get the sensation at all. But he did want to encourage her change in mood. "There, see? We agree on something."

They stood on opposite sides of the small gate, her fingers locked over the top in a death grip. She shook her head as she looked at him.

"Garrett." That's all she said. His name in that deep voice that drove him wild.

"Let's go inside and we'll figure this out."

She hesitated for another second before stepping back and gesturing for him to follow her up the steps. "I suppose you think this is an official date."

Compared to what they had been doing before tonight, they were practically engaged. "We picked up dinner. We're going into your house together. You're right. Clearly not a date."

He ignored the idea of her having a husband and this amounting to cheating. In his head, whatever she had with Carl was long over. He just hoped she felt the same way.

"You think you're so clever." Amusement filled her voice.

He loved when she entered into verbal volleys with him. When the edge fell away and it was just them talking. "I'm going to be humble here and let you be the one to throw around descriptions like *clever. Brilliant.*

Whatever means always being right. I think we can agree those fit."

She rolled her eyes as she slid her key in the lock. "You never disappoint."

"Let's hope you hold on to that thought as we continue to date."

"I never said . . ." She opened the door but didn't even cross the threshold before slamming to a halt. "Oh, my God."

The tremble in her voice hit him first. The lights were on, just as they left them. He didn't hear a sound but he rushed to put his body in front of hers. That's when he saw them. Men's deck shoes. The legs.

A guy on her floor.

"What the fuck?" Garrett shot inside and held out a hand to keep her back. A quick check of the house, looking behind doors and scanning every inch for signs of struggle or a break-in, then he was back at her side.

Ignoring his warning, she'd walked up to the body and stared down with a face that had gone pale. Her gaze traveled all over the motionless form.

"Carl?" His name came out as a whisper as she started to slide to her knees beside him.

Garrett caught her just in time. "No."

She looked ready to go around him if necessary. "But he's—"

"Stop." Garrett knew what Carl was. The still body, the unmoving chest and an expanding blood pool. Yeah, he recognized the signs. "Call 9–1–1. Use your cell."

She fumbled with her phone, nearly dropped it as she grabbed it out of her jeans pocket. The extra seconds gave Garrett a chance to lean down and check for a pulse. He went through the motions but he knew he didn't have to.

He could hear her talking, begging for an ambulance. The stream of words stopped as she tore her gaze away from Carl's body to look at Garrett. "Is he okay?"

She had to be in shock because she was too smart to ask that question. Worse, he couldn't figure out a decent way to answer. "Uh, not really."

"What does that mean?"

Garrett prided himself on handling difficult situations. He balanced work issues and talked to people all day. His boss and best friend, Wren, wasn't great with other humans, so it often fell to Garrett to explain things and deliver bad news.

But nothing had prepared him for this, for the panic in her eyes or the way her hands shook. He hated being the one who delivered the news. "He's dead, Lauren."

She almost dropped the phone. "He can't be."

"This time he really is."

Chapter Three

GARRETT STOOD TO the side of Lauren's living room with his friend Matthias Clarke and looked over at Carl's body. Time seemed to blur and bend but Garrett guessed almost two hours had passed since the discovery. The bag of Thai food sat unopened on the counter as the forensic and police teams worked the room. The small space was alive with activity and noise.

"I hate when the dead don't stay dead," Matthias said in his typical deadpan voice. He'd been called in from his new house, the one he shared with Lauren's best friend, Kayla, about twenty minutes away. It was late but Matthias still wore a suit and tie . . . because of course he did. The guy owned a security company and lived his life as if he were permanently on call.

"Lower your voice." Garrett glanced across the room

to the kitchen where Lauren stood, answering questions about Carl's brother and anyone else who might need to be contacted. "But yeah."

Matthias crossed his arms in front of him. At six-four he was formidable enough that seasoned police officers with impressive weapons on display gave him room when they walked by. "So this fucker appears out of nowhere after thirty or so months, makes demands and then shows up bleeding out on her floor."

That's one of the many things Garrett liked about Matthias. The guy didn't pick and choose his words. He just plowed ahead. Matthias and Garrett's boss and friend, Wren, spent a lot of years together in their twenties. Garrett knew Matthias through Wren. Garrett actually knew a whole group of guys who once called themselves the Quint Five in deference to the mentor who took them all in and saved them from everything ranging from prison to sure death.

He trusted all of them. None of them knew he'd been dating—or not dating, depending on who you asked—Lauren, but they would soon. Matthias would see to that. Talking shit would come in waves after that. Garrett seriously considered throwing away his cell.

"I should probably remind you to show some respect for the dead, but damn, I hate this guy." A kick of guilt smacked into Garrett as he said the words. Carl's body wasn't even cold but with the way the guy had lived his life, Garrett didn't have any trouble imagining someone wanting him dead.

"*Hated.*" Matthias made an odd sound. "And maybe don't volunteer that information."

"Why?" Garrett asked, half listening to Matthias while keeping tuned into the conversation Lauren was having. He really wanted a lawyer with her, but she seemed to be holding up just fine, not giving one bit of important information away.

Damn, he loved smart women.

"You're dating Carl's ex and happen to be in town rather than on your planned trip to California right when said ex rises from the dead and someone slams him in the head with a cast-iron frying pan." Matthias's voice dropped lower, inching as close to a whisper as Matthias ever got. "There's a word for what you're about to become here."

"Clue me in."

"*Suspect.*"

"Oh, come on." Garrett tried to scoff the idea away but it settled in his brain. He hadn't even kissed Lauren yet and he could wind up as the target of police interest. Wasn't that just fucking great? "But we're barely . . ."

"Yes?" Matthias put a finger behind his ear and leaned in. "What words are you looking for? Sleeping together? Dating? See, I'm your best friend—"

"You're actually not." Wren was, but even Garrett had to admit that Matthias had grown on him. The gruffness, the demanding nature, how stupid in love he was with Kayla and how fast he fell. It was hard not to like the guy.

"—and I didn't know you and Lauren had a thing. Imagine what the police are going to think. Add in the absence of a break-in and the presence of the murder weapon, which appears to be the bloodstained pan in the sink, and you've got a perception problem." Matthias smiled, which was never a great sign for the person on the receiving end of it. "Lucky for you, Wren found another way of helping."

Wren worked miracles but the slamming in Garrett's gut didn't ease. "How?"

Matthias nodded in the general direction of the older man, the only one not in uniform, coming in Lauren's front door. "Detective Rick Cryer."

Garrett knew him, had worked with him before on the case where Wren met his girlfriend, Emery. "He's retired."

This wasn't his jurisdiction or even his job. Thanks to the media firestorm following Emery's case, Detective Cryer was now considered a cold-case specialist and in high demand. Garrett couldn't imagine how many favors and how much maneuvering and ego-stroking Wren had done to get a friendly ear like Cryer on this case.

"I guess you owe Wren."

Understatement. Garrett owed Wren—all of the Quint Five—for a lot more than this. "He should just clear me, so we can get on with finding out what really happened here."

"Any clues?"

"None. I've heard mumbling that the area around

the body and in the kitchen had been wiped free of fingerprints, including Lauren's, which should logically be in her own house. She has an alarm and locks and someone got around all of it."

Matthias exhaled. "Well, I think Cryer would be more amenable to making your presence here go away quietly if we weren't also dealing with the dead guy's former silent business partner, his brother and his girlfriend, the same woman Carl left Lauren for."

That last part struck Garrett as out of place with Carl's insistence he be allowed to move back in with Lauren. "That woman is in town?"

"Yes, as are the other two. Apparently all three of them are demanding answers."

"Great." Garrett's mind flipped to the people he saw huddled outside. Some were neighbors. Others demanded to speak with someone in charge. He'd bet at least one of them had a vested interest in Carl.

"How's Lauren?" Matthias asked.

Garrett's gaze traveled back to her, toured her face. Exhaustion tugged at the corner of her mouth. The shock still hadn't left her wide eyes. "Stunned."

"Understandable. It's not every day a supposedly dead husband shows up really dead—re-dead, dead again . . . I'm actually not sure of the proper terminology here—on her carpet." Matthias said something under his breath that sounded a lot like *the stupid fucker*.

"I'm thinking he'll only really be dead this one time." And he deserved justice, so Garrett vowed to get it for him. For Lauren, really, but Garrett was fine with Carl benefitting in some small way from that.

"Good. It would suck if this kept happening."

Garrett barely heard the words but then the comment hit him full force. "Was that a joke?"

Matthias shrugged. "Kind of."

"The whole girlfriend thing suits you." Garrett took the opportunity to sneak a peek at Kayla. She hovered right behind Lauren as they shook hands with Detective Cryer.

Kayla had been a surprise. Garrett had come to Annapolis with Matthias months ago at Wren's urging to learn more about Matthias's brother's murder years before. The sexy waitress with the reddish-brown hair knocked Matthias right off his game and Garrett had loved every minute of watching the big man fall.

"You have no idea." Matthias's wide grin came and went. "But, one warning for you. Kayla is Lauren's best friend. You might want to remember that."

"Meaning?"

"Don't fuck Lauren over. Kayla might look sweet but she will break you in half if you hurt Lauren." Matthias shook his head. "She's got a mean streak and her love for Lauren is absolute."

"I know firsthand how tough Kayla is." She'd actually saved his life months ago, which was not something Garrett was likely to forget. "Besides, if she can tolerate you she must have nerves of steel."

"You've been warned."

A few minutes later Lauren headed for them with Kayla trailing right behind her. She kept walking until she stood next to Garrett. When she leaned against him, he wrapped an arm around her and pressed a palm against her lower back. If she needed support, he was more than willing to provide it.

"Hey." Her smile didn't reach her eyes.

She was tall, almost five-nine, but he still had a good four inches on her. Still, for the first time ever, she slumped. Seemed vulnerable when she usually radiated strength. "You okay?"

"Not really."

"Yeah, I guess not," Matthias said as his gaze switched from Garrett to Lauren and back again.

Lauren never stopped moving. She shifted her weight and bit her lip as she talked to her friends. "Thanks for coming."

"We'll be here for whatever you need." Kayla reached out and grabbed Lauren's hand.

Lauren held on for a few seconds then dropped her hand. "Right now, I just need to sit down. The endless questioning has my head spinning."

"What are the police saying?" Matthias asked in his usual cut-through-the-bullshit kind of way.

"That I can't leave town."

Garrett wasn't surprised. "Standard procedure."

Lauren glanced up at him. "You mean there is a set way of handling a situation where someone comes back from the dead?"

The woman had a point. "Admittedly, this might be uncharted territory."

"You can come back to the house and stay with us for as long as you need to." Kayla reached for Lauren's arm as if to lead her toward the front door.

Garrett pounced. He didn't mean to, but his voice rose and he instinctively stepped in front of Lauren. "No."

"Interesting. Do you have another suggestion, Garrett?"

Garrett ignored the amusement he heard in Matthias's voice and saw in Kayla's raised eyebrow as he answered. "I got her a suite at the Carsley Inn."

For a second the rest of the group stared at him. If there was such a thing as a group frown he could now honestly say he'd been on the receiving end of one. The women managed to look baffled and skeptical. Matthias clearly fought off a smile. The asshole.

"This suite . . ." Matthias's annoyingly light voice trailed off. "You'll just happen to be sleeping in it as well?"

That was enough to break Kayla's stare. She rolled her eyes. "Subtle."

"I can stay here." Lauren looked around, her gaze bouncing off the walls and furniture—everywhere but at Carl and the experts buzzing around his body, collecting evidence and taking photographs of everything and everyone.

"It's a crime scene. You have to leave for at least a short time." Garrett wanted to get her out of there. That meant heading through the crowd outside and possibly being stopped by someone who knew Carl.

"My office—"

"Lauren." She still wasn't getting this, so he tried again. "This isn't up for debate."

Fire flashed in her eyes. "Excuse me?"

About damn time. There was the Lauren he knew. Sharp, aware and not easy to push around. The last few hours had beaten her down but she rose right back up again. Garrett couldn't think of anything hotter.

Matthias leaned closer to Kayla but didn't bother lowering his voice. "Watching these two work through this is going to be fun."

Lauren's head shot up. "This?"

The tone suggested she was not in the mood for jokes. If Matthias heard it, he ignored it. "Do I really have to spell it out?"

Kayla sighed at him. "A man is dead."

"Right." Matthias cleared his throat. "Sorry."

That led them right back to Garrett's point. He wanted to get settled in, call Wren and try to get a read on Detective Cryer's initial thoughts on the case. First, he had to convince Lauren she needed a roommate. "Matthias and Kayla don't live in town. You need to be close to work and available for . . . questioning."

Kayla winced. "Not your best argument since I work twenty feet away from her office."

A man could not catch a break. Garrett wanted to tell both Matthias and Kayla that he could handle this, but he was pretty sure Kayla would punch him. He spared her a quick glance before looking at Lauren again. She was the one he needed to convince. "My point is the Carsley Inn is a neutral location. We can watch over you there. I'll be nearby."

Matthias shook his head. "We're finally getting to a bit of truth."

"Shut up," Garrett shot back.

"It's not fun having your personal life picked apart, is it?" Matthias asked. "Having a friend all up in your dating business."

Lauren frowned at Matthias. "We're not dating."

It figured that was the part of the conversation she'd focus on. Garrett couldn't imagine what Matthias would do with that information later.

"Are you sure?" Matthias asked.

Lauren's frown only deepened. "Wouldn't I know?"

"Given Garrett's skill with women? Possibly not."

"Okay, stop. Let's focus." Garrett moved Lauren out of the direct path from the front door to the body as two members of the forensic team headed for Detective Cryer. Garrett tried to ignore all the activity spinning around them and focus on the woman in front of him. "Come to the Inn for a few days. I'll ride the detective to get you back into the house as soon as possible."

"And where will you be while all of this happens?" Matthias asked.

Garrett didn't even look at his friend. He kept staring at Lauren, willing her to agree. "On her couch. For protection."

Matthias exhaled. "Of course. Who wouldn't want a finance guy as a bodyguard?"

Oh, come on. "Do you even know what I do?"

Matthias shrugged. "Not really."

Garrett was about to shoot off a two-word response when Lauren answered. "Fine."

Kayla's eyes widened. "What?"

"You're making it too easy on him, Lauren," Matthias said at the same time.

"I don't want to put either of you in danger, especially so soon after all that happened to you." Lauren's voice grew stronger the more she talked to Kayla.

"You're saying you're okay with Garrett being in danger?" Matthias got the question out but Kayla elbowed him in the stomach right after.

"Let me get the okay from Detective Cryer and we can leave." Lauren headed back to the kitchen before Garrett could stop her.

As soon as she was gone Kayla pointed at Garrett. "You behave."

"What are you—"

A sharp shake of her head stopped him from saying anything else. "Garrett, her idiot husband is dead—"

"Again," Matthias added.

Kayla talked right over him. "She is on a wild emotional ride. Don't add to it."

"Did we stop getting along and you didn't tell me?" Back when she started dating Matthias, Garrett had been her ally. An ally to both of them, really, but they didn't know that at the time.

"I like when you keep Matthias in line."

Matthias threw his hands up in the air. "Hey."

"But I'm not sure if I want you crawling all over my best friend." Lauren's eyes narrowed. "I've seen how you look at her. All those trips down here for *pie*. Please. As if they don't serve pie in DC."

Not pie that came with a view of Lauren, but Garrett decided not to explain that. Not when Kayla was in protective momma-bear mode.

"I don't plan to . . ." But he stopped because he actually did plan to. Not right now because he had some level of control and decency, but he didn't have any plans to leave Lauren alone unless she asked him to. And he sure as hell hoped that didn't happen. "Okay, I do have some finesse, you know."

Kayla studied him for a second. Her half-angry, half-skeptical gaze roamed all over him. "Then use it. Lauren might be tough on the outside but Carl is her weak spot."

"She's not in love with him." He was positive that much was true.

"He hurt her, Garrett." Kayla's voice dropped lower. "You better not do the same."

Chapter Four

IT TOOK THEM another hour to pack up the few things the police let Lauren take, answer a few more questions and get out of there. Checking into the suite ran smoother. Then the pacing started. She walked back and forth in front of the small couch in the living room area and tried to clear her head. Looking at the one king-sized bed hadn't done it. That took her mind in another, very wild direction.

This might be the right place, but it was not a reasonable time. Carl was dead. The police were asking questions. But still, the revving inside her wouldn't stop. It was as if energy pinged around, begging to escape. She felt as if she were out of control and careening toward some invisible edge.

The only thing that made sense to her right now was Garrett. Strong, reliable, oh-so-tempting Garrett.

She'd held him off for months but he kept coming back. At first, his tenacity weirded her out. Not that she thought he was dangerous. She just didn't get why he bothered. The man was tall and fit with shoulders she ached to climb. He'd shoot her a smile and her insides would melt. Turn her into one big puddle of longing and need.

Back then she'd been so careful. She might have convinced the court Carl was dead but she knew better. The lingering worry he'd be back never left her mind. She'd never been a lucky person. She'd gone from taking care of a mother who battled depression and darkness with pills and alcohol, until the day she followed through with her threats to drive her car into that tree, to a husband who demanded she handle all the physical work while he kept her at an emotional distance. It was quieter, safer, to be alone.

Out on the boat. Laughing with clients. None of that was real. She could leave it behind at the end of the day and not be responsible for anyone else's happiness or health.

Then Garrett stormed into her life.

He was funny and charming and made no secret about how much he wanted her. He whipped her up in this storm and she'd never experienced anything like it. She took wealthy successful people out on the boat all the time. They tried to impress her. A few idiot men even attempted to touch her. One "accidentally" landed in the water and to this day believed he got there because he slipped and was grateful to her for fishing him out. She knew that because he continued to recommend her boating expertise to friends and business acquaintances.

Garrett didn't fit that mold at all. He was confident without being an asshole. Up until him she had thought those two things were irrevocably linked.

She watched him now as he set their bags down next to the bed. Her first thought was that she actually liked him. The second had to do with how much she missed sex and was ready to restart that part of her life even though the thought of caring about anyone, even short term, scared her witless.

All of those thoughts ran through her head but she went with a more neutral topic. "Did Kayla give you the shovel talk?"

He glanced over at her with that sexy grin that made her knees buckle. "What?"

"The 'hurt her and I'll bury you in the desert' shovel talk."

He hummed as he nodded. "Sort of."

"She's being overprotective. It's sweet."

He frowned. "I wonder why."

"Me, too."

He treated her to one of those long-suffering male exhales. "I was being sarcastic." He walked over to her and ran a hand up and down her arm. "Hey, sit for a second."

"You got a room with one bed." Nothing like stating the obvious, but there it was.

"It's a suite. I plan on sleeping on the couch."

"You don't have to." The words popped out and sat there in the roaring silence.

She sure did know how to kill a conversation.

"I think that . . ." His hand dropped to his side as his eyes narrowed. "Wait, what?"

In the history of sex conversations this might not be the easiest one. It sure didn't fill her with confidence to have to beg him to understand her.

Those hands and that almost unbearable hotness— she got the sense Garrett McGrath knew what to do with a woman. That made the wide-eyed, openmouthed stare he kept sending her even odder. No way he lacked experience. Everything about him telegraphed sex. Since she didn't think it was from a lack of interest either, she tried again. "We can share the bed."

"I want to make sure we're not experiencing a misunderstanding here." He hesitated between each word, as if giving her a chance to jump in and stop him.

Then his mouth kicked up in a grin and relief whooshed through her. For all his talk, he *got* it, or at least he was starting to. "I don't think we are."

He held up a hand but the confused look had vanished. No, the emotion in his eyes could only be described as explosive interest. "Okay, tell me what's happening right now? Use small words. I'll keep up."

"I'm all churned up and pissed off." She started

to pace, or she would have if he hadn't been standing *right there*. One step and she ran into him, had to put a hand on his chest to steady herself. "It's been a long time . . ."

"Since?"

He had to be playing with her now. "Are you really this slow?"

His hand covered hers. That thumb brushed over the back of her hand in a gesture so sexy and soft that she almost jumped on him.

"You're talking about sex." His voice dipped lower now, right into the it's-time-to-get-naked range.

Took him long enough. "Yes, Garrett. Hot, strip-our-clothes-off, climb-on-the-bed sex. Or against the wall. I don't care how as long as it happens. With you."

That last part seemed important so she added it. It took mindless sex and plunged it to a deeper level, but she didn't care. It was the truth. She wanted him. Specifically, him.

His hand froze and he visibly swallowed. "You refused to have anything we could even call a dinner date for three months and now you want to get naked?"

"Yes."

"You do know I've visited you nonstop since we first met, right? This is the first green light, if that's what it is, I've gotten."

He really was going to make her spell this out. "It's a green light. It's not going to get any greener."

Still he didn't move. They stood there, staring at each

other in the silent room. The only sound came from the clicking on and off of the heater.

A minute ticked by and then, without a word, he put his hands on either side of her waist and pulled her in closer. The touch scorched her. Everywhere their bodies met—their chests, thighs—her skin burned. She ached with the need to wrap her body around his and just hold on.

"Clue me in here, Lauren." His voice sounded rough and raspy now. "I mean, fuck yes, the answer is yes anytime you want. But why now? Why the change? I need to know that we're not going to be dealing with regrets tomorrow on top of everything else you have to handle right now."

She couldn't hold eye contact. For a second, her gaze bounced around the room from the pristine white comforter to the velvet drapes covering the floor-to-ceiling windows and pooling on the floor. "It's ridiculous, I know."

"I sure as hell didn't say that."

The amusement in his voice had her looking at him again. Her gaze met his and something inside her tumbled. It was as if her stomach flipped over and kept spinning. "I have all this energy bouncing around inside me. My mind is scrambled and I teeter between being so pissed off I want to punch something and feeling guilty and half sick that Carl died that way."

Garrett rested his forehead against hers. "I'm sorry."

"I'm confused and feel sad for him. For those who

care about him." She didn't mean to dampen the mood, but she did need to say the words. Just once.

"Are you excluding yourself?"

She pulled back to look at him again. "What?"

"You're not in love with him."

There was no need to lie about this. She actually didn't want to cover up anything when it came to Garrett. Something about him tugged at her, made her want to tell him her secrets and restart the life she'd convinced herself she could never have.

Stick to work had been her motto for so long. But now, just for a few nights, she wanted something else. Something that was just hers. Something private and real.

"I haven't been for a long time." She toyed with the band at the v-neck of Garrett's sweater. "But I've spent these last few years hating him and now I think about what his final minutes must have been like and—"

"Okay. Let's try this." One of Garrett's hands came up to cup her face. "Breathe."

The gentle touch soothed her. She leaned into his palm and let herself slip into the sensation of skin against skin. "I think I just want to feel something."

"It sounds like you're feeling a lot."

He understood. Maybe that was the piece that made all the difference. He didn't judge her actions or what she did to push Carl away. No, the voices in her head took care of that.

"But none of it is healthy and nothing is within my

control," she said, thinking about the anger that had boiled up inside her when Carl came to her door.

"I am."

"Meaning?" She silently hoped they'd finally landed on the same page.

"I'm here for whatever you need. Protection. Someone to listen." His thumb slipped over her bottom lip. "Someone to touch you. A body to explore."

Her breath hiccupped in her chest. She had to fight to find enough air to talk. "I've tried so hard to stay away from you."

"Why is that exactly?" He leaned in until his breath blew across her cheek.

His hands moved to her back and his leg slid between hers. The roughness of his black pants seemed to penetrate her jeans. Her mind scrambled at the intimate contact.

"I don't know." Her breathy voice hung between them.

"I think you do."

She didn't want to talk about this. Not now. But something about the way he coaxed and supported had her spilling the secrets she'd kept locked inside. "Because I knew Carl was alive. I lied to the courts and anyone who needed to hear me say he was dead, but I knew."

His lips skimmed her forehead then her nose. "There you go."

Some of the Carl-related tension seeped out of her. "You knew that already?"

"You rebuilt a boating business and brought it back from bankruptcy, all while earning the trust of the men in your field and handling idiot clients." His mouth hovered right over hers. "I was pretty sure you could identify a con man once it was clear he was one."

"You were right." She wanted to reach out, tip her head. Get closer. "I suspected all along. More than that, I could feel it. I knew he was alive and screwing with me."

His hand slipped behind her neck, cradling her head. "I've been wanting you to say that since the first day we met."

"I didn't kill him." She whispered the words because she needed him to know. "I rushed you out for a walk in the cold when you first got there, never letting you in the house. Someone might think that's suspect but I need you to know I didn't kill him and use you as an alibi."

"I didn't think you did." He made a sexy little humming sound as he kissed her temple. "You are strong and have this thing where you stay quiet and assess and analyze from a distance."

Her stomach dropped and she started to step back. "I'm aloof."

"You're a lot of things, Lauren." Those strong arms held her in place. "You're not aloof and you're not a killer."

She stopped trying to pull away. "And you'd know about the latter."

"I've known a lot of killers."

He'd dropped comments like that before but never followed up. She knew she should ask a bunch of questions but there was something comforting about the fact that he'd seen awful things and hadn't changed. They didn't harden him. For now, knowing that was enough. "That should scare me, but it doesn't."

"Further proof we'll be good together."

Her gaze dipped to his mouth. To that soft bit of sexy scruff around his mouth. "We should see."

He answered by lowering his head. His mouth touched hers as his fingers plunged into her hair. One touch of his lips and any worries she had fell away. The kiss swept her up and whipped her around. She felt light-headed and almost drunk from the force of it. Heat raced through her veins and her fingers clenched his arms. She couldn't get close enough or hold him tight enough.

She didn't realize they'd moved across the room until her back hit the wall. The thud echoed through her. He reached down and slipped his hand over her thigh. It was all the coaxing she needed. She wrapped her leg around his and her ankle slid up and down his calf.

Heat thrummed off him. A growing bulge pressed against her. Need washed over her.

Their hands traveled and the blinding kiss roared on. Every muscle snapped to life. All that pent-up need exploded inside her. And when his hand went to her breast, cupping her, caressing her through her sweater, she fought to gulp in enough air.

Their heavy breathing floated through the room and a sexy little grumble sounded in his throat. When she arched her back and pressed her middle against him, the grumble morphed to a rumbling moan. She had never heard anything sexier.

His mouth slipped to her cheek then to that sensitive spot right behind her ear. She grabbed fistfuls of his shirt and yanked, desperate to touch skin to skin.

"God, yes. Lauren . . ." His hot mouth pressed against her throat, forcing her head back.

A rush of adrenaline had her pulling and tugging on his shirt. "Why are you still dressed?"

His laugh vibrated against her collarbone as his mouth dipped lower. "I can fix that in about two seconds."

She palmed his cheeks and lifted his head so she could see those sexy eyes. The intensity of his gaze stole her breath. He did nothing to hide his emotions. Need, desire, heat . . . it was all right there.

"Now, Lauren."

She closed the brief slip of space between them and brushed her mouth over his. "Yes."

Just as he deepened the kiss, a banging started in her head. She pulled back and tried to identify the sound.

"Who is at the damn door?" Garrett slowly dropped his hands. "Wait here."

His words ripped her right out of the fantasy and dunked her back into the real world. Slowly the room tilted to rights again and the sounds and smells of the hotel came zooming back to her. Then his words hit her.

"Not going to happen." As if she were going to start following his orders. She walked right behind him across the room, ignoring the frown he sent her way. "Technically it's my room."

"It's in my name," he shot back, not bothering to lower his voice.

He looked through the peephole and swore under his breath. Before she could ask, he gestured for her to take a turn.

"Jake." She mouthed the word, barely making a sound.

Garrett swore again as he pulled down his sweater and put his clothes back in order. "I'm starting to hate everyone in your late husband's family."

She unlocked the door. "You'll like Jake."

"Probably not now that I know you do."

GARRETT FORCED HIS breathing to return to normal as she opened the door. The last thing he wanted was a visitor. Especially one related to Carl. But really, anyone. Not after he'd finally kissed her.

What the hell had he been waiting for? All those wasted months.

The taste and smell of her. The feel of her mouth

against his. The way she grabbed on to him. Even now he could feel the bite of her fingernails through his sweater. All he wanted to do was kick this Jake guy out and get her into bed. Then keep her there.

The brother stumbled in. His breathing was labored and his gaze immediately latched on to her. "Lauren, I—"

"Hello." That's all it took to turn the guy's attention. Now that Garrett had it, he came to one easy but annoying conclusion—he hated Jake on sight.

Garrett knew from the intel he'd gathered on Carl and his family over the last few months that Jake was four years younger than Carl. Only a month's difference separated his age from Lauren's. Jake also was taller than Carl, lankier and very single. Not to mention blonder with objective good looks that could place him in any city bar with a swarm of younger women around him.

He'd been married and divorced young. He held some sort of lower-level management job. Garrett didn't care about any of that. He did care about the way he stared at Lauren. That was a problem because there was nothing brotherly about it. His gaze had traveled over her, hesitating on her breasts before returning to her face. Garrett didn't have a brother, but he couldn't imagine looking at a brother's wife or girlfriend like that.

"The guy from DC, right?" Jake held out his hand.

Garrett was tempted not to shake it but he wasn't a total dick. Still, he glanced at Lauren for confirmation. "Is that how you describe me to other people?"

She ignored him as she ushered Jake inside. "Are you okay?"

Garrett didn't see that all the touching was necessary, but the guy had just lost his brother. Garrett was willing to refrain from punching him for that reason alone.

"I . . . We just got him back and now—" Jake's words cut off as he shook his head.

Grief washed over the room. Jake's voice was scratchy and his movements slow. Guilt punched into Garrett. Here he was hating the guy for his obvious crush on his sister-in-law and Jake was in mourning. Separating out all that had happened over the last few hours from how much he despised what Carl did to Lauren was harder than Garrett expected.

Garrett gave voice to the question burning in his mind. "How did you know we were here?"

He hadn't shared that information with anyone but Wren, Matthias and Kayla. Detective Cryer had probably guessed since he was staying down the hall and they passed him when they checked in. They'd exchanged a few words that convinced Garrett the detective knew Lauren wasn't his answer.

Garrett couldn't imagine any of those people broadcasting the information about Lauren's location. Not when a murderer was on the loose and the potential danger to her was still unclear.

"I'm sorry, your name is?" Jake asked with a frown.

"Garrett." He admired the other man's stalling tactic. He dodged right around the question without trouble.

"I'm Jake, Carl's brother." Jake turned back to Lauren. He took a step, closing the gap between them. "I needed to come over and talk with you."

Uh-huh. Garrett doubled back to the obvious question. "Again, how did you know where to look?"

Jake barely spared Garrett a glance. "The police told me."

Not likely. Garrett filed that information away for later.

Lauren walked Jake over to the couch. "Sit."

"Lauren . . ." Jake shook his head and he propped his elbows on his knees. "What happened to Carl?"

She sat down next to him. "I have no idea."

Garrett watched their interaction. She delivered every move and every word like she always did—clear and uncomplicated. Jake stared at her, his gaze following her as if he were hanging on each word.

"I know the two of you fought earlier."

She shook her head. "Jake, I didn't—"

"Oh, I know." He sat up straighter and slipped his hand over hers where it rested on her knee. "What I really was asking about was what happened to Carl out there, during those years he was gone."

"He didn't tell you?" She leaned back into the cushion, sliding her hand along her thigh and out of Jake's hold.

It was a subtle move. Impressive. Whatever Jake felt for Lauren clearly wasn't reciprocated. That's all that mattered to Garrett. That and the answer to how far Jake would go to feed this obvious crush. The idea that he might have taken out his own brother to grab his wife was almost Shakespearean in its sickness.

"He wouldn't talk. It was as if he thought he could pick up his life as though nothing happened." Jake talked with his hands. "It didn't make any sense."

Lauren nodded. "I got that impression from him, too."

"What about the girlfriend?" Garrett asked, cutting through the bullshit as quickly as possible. He knew his original evening plans were over thanks to the visit, but that didn't mean he wanted to spend the night listening to this guy.

Jake's gaze shot to Lauren and he winced. "Maybe we should—"

Lauren waved him off. "There's no need to hide it. It's not as if I don't know about her."

"Maryanne is here." Jake glanced at his hands then back up at Lauren. "In town."

That was interesting in a what-the-fuck kind of way. Garrett couldn't believe the woman hadn't skipped town, though she might have by now. If Lauren fell under suspicion, so would the other woman. "Were they still together?"

"No, he was clear he wanted Lauren back."

"Sounds like someone needs to talk with Maryanne." Garrett wanted that to happen before the woman wised up and ran.

Jake frowned at Garrett. "Why?"

"Right now she might be the only one with answers." And Garrett wanted to know them as soon as possible.

Chapter Five

THE NEXT MORNING Kayla sat with Lauren in her office. They sipped on their takeout coffee cups from the diner down the pier where Kayla worked. That's how they met more than a year ago. Due to proximity and over a shared love of bad horror movies.

Kayla was on a break as they both were most days at this time when Lauren wasn't out on the boat, which was most of the time in the winter. They both kicked back, using Lauren's desk as a footrest.

"So . . ." Kayla stared at Lauren over the top of her cup.

Lauren knew from one syllable where the conversation was headed. She'd spent a good portion of the night thinking about him, listening to him breathe from the couch on the other side of the room and wishing Jake hadn't shown up and killed the mood. "Nope."

"Hey!" Kayla banged her heel against the desk. "You and Garrett. Talk."

"Still no."

"I knew about the trips down here, but yesterday when you needed someone to handle Carl, you texted Garrett." Lauren wiggled her eyebrows. "That seems big."

Very, but Lauren refused to admit that.

She sat up, letting her feet fall to the floor. "We aren't going to become those women who only talk about men, are we?"

"Couldn't we be them just long enough for you to give me the scoop on what happened in the inn?"

The pleading in Kayla's voice made Lauren laugh. "There's nothing to tell."

"I can't believe Garrett let a solid opportunity pass him by. He seems like he'd be smooth. Good with his hands, if you know what I mean."

Oh, she definitely did.

"His skills are fine. Trust me." When Kayla started to say something, Lauren cut her off. "And that's all you get for now."

"You are so infuriating."

"But you love me."

Kayla drained the rest of her cup before setting it down on the edge of the desk. "Unconditionally."

And she meant it. With so much of Lauren's life revolving around chance and problems, Kayla was the one person she could count on. They talked. They hung out. They shared meals. They gossiped about the other people who worked on the pier and complained about the customers and the quirks that worked on their nerves.

Not that long ago one of Lauren's big-money sailing-lesson clients had turned out to be someone other than who he pretended to be and tried to kill both Kayla and Garrett. The guilt from that day kept Lauren paralyzed for weeks. Neither of them had blamed her, so she'd decided to blame herself in their place.

"We should . . ." The rest of the sentence, whatever it was, disappeared from Lauren's head as soon as the words trailed off. The figure in the doorway had her sputtering as she tried to remember anything other than Carl's deceit.

"May I come in? Just for a minute."

At the sound of the woman's soft voice, Kayla dropped her feet to the floor and spun around to face the door.

Now they were all staring at each other. Lauren had wondered what she'd do when or if she ever met the woman Carl had run off with. Now she knew. She'd shut down, afraid that talking might lead to babbling. Her head would pound and the whole world would close in on her until every sound became muffled.

She used the silence to study the woman Carl had found so enticing. The one who helped him commit fraud and take a wrecking ball to her life. Lauren had seen photos. After all, when Carl disappeared, so did Maryanne. Her family and friends had grieved. Now she stood there, five-six or so and petite. Brown hair and brown eyes. Pretty in her oversized Nordic print sweater and down vest.

She also looked terrified. Her gaze darted around the room and wariness showed in every inch of her face. She was younger—of course. She'd been twenty-four when they'd taken off for their pretend drowning. Lauren could only hope the other woman was wiser now.

"Maryanne, this is my friend Kayla."

Kayla's eyes bulged as she stood up. "Whoa."

"Wait." Maryanne held up her hands as if in mock surrender. "I'm not here to fight. I swear."

Lauren was pretty sure she was the one with the right to kick and scream, but okay. "Come in."

She stood up then couldn't remember why she'd done that and immediately sank back down in her chair again. With her fingers wrapped around the armrests, she waited for the anger to hit. Maryanne had walked away without debt. Even her college loans had been paid off by Carl.

Maryanne also got Carl . . . though Lauren wasn't completely sure the other woman had won on that score.

"What are you doing here?" Lauren had a thousand questions but that seemed like a good place to start.

"I'm sorry," Maryanne blurted out.

Lauren could see Maryanne drag in a long breath. Tears filled her eyes but she blinked them away. The woman rubbed her hands together until her skin turned red. Then it hit Lauren . . . Maryanne might actually have loved Carl. He'd run away with her and come back yesterday professing to be home. Lauren had no idea what happened in between but she guessed it hadn't been great for Maryanne. It's not as if Carl changed into a better man while he was gone. His visit to her proved that.

"For what?" Kayla asked the question with a bit of an edge.

Maryanne flinched but didn't come out fighting or run away. Lauren reluctantly admired that sort of spirit. She'd spent a lot of time hating this woman she only knew in photos. Now that Maryanne stood there, looking like she was held together with little more than rubber bands and spit, looming on the verge of breaking down, Lauren couldn't muster any anger.

"I didn't know." Maryanne swallowed, and when she spoke again her voice was louder. "He told me you were separated. When we started dating, I mean."

"Did he also tell you he planned to fake his death or did he spring that on you once you were out on the water?" Kayla asked.

Lauren didn't jump in and fix this for Maryanne. She'd made her decisions, including the one to walk into the office. Tears or not, she'd helped turn Lauren's life upside down and Lauren was not ready to forgive that.

Maryanne nodded. "I thought we were running away together. Then, once we were out on the water, he talked about the money and how he wanted out from under the debt. He said . . ."

"What?" Lauren hated to ask but the not knowing would kill her.

"He said you ran up bills he had no ability to pay and . . . honestly, he never said a good thing about you."

"To his mistress?" Kayla snorted. "Go figure."

"I didn't know he was lying."

Lauren decided not to remind Maryanne about his big lie, the one about dying. She leaned forward with her elbows on the desk and silently begged the wrenching in her stomach to stop. "What happened once you were away from here, Maryanne?"

"At first it was great." She blew out a shaky breath. "Then he got . . . weird. Mean."

Lauren knew the real answer. "When the money ran out."

She knew how his mind worked. Money translated to calm for him. When the amount he stole from the business and their accounts was gone, he would have become accusatory and shitty. That described most of her life with him during the last few years of their marriage.

Kayla's eyes narrowed. "You came back with him. So did you think you were going to tell some wild story about being lost and then start over here?"

Maryanne winced. "He disappeared three weeks ago."

"Weeks?" Kayla looked at Lauren. "Where has he been for all that time?"

"In hiding? I don't know but it's a good question."

Maryanne's words came rushing back to Lauren. "You said 'disappeared.' You mean he left you behind?"

"In the Bahamas. Without a penny." Maryanne glanced down before facing Lauren again. "It took me some time to figure out . . . you know. That he wasn't coming back. Then I had to get the money together . . . He took the bit I had saved while waitressing there."

Kayla whistled. "Man, he was a jackass."

"What happened to him once he got back here? I read this morning . . . Then the police came to see me . . ."

The woman liked to talk in sentence fragments. Lauren chalked it up to Maryanne's strained emotional state. She got it. She had been the same way when Carl first left. Seeing his body on the floor yesterday had sent a renewed shot of anguish through her but it vanished as soon as it came.

The guilt, the confusion—they would always be with her. The love died long ago, along with the trust.

"Someone killed him." Despite everything, it still hurt Lauren to say the words.

Maryanne continued to hover by the door. She'd stepped inside but not far. "He died in your house."

Kayla shook her head. "It wasn't her, if that's what you're trying not to ask."

"It really wasn't." Lauren's heart raced. It was as if the anxiety built up inside her whenever she thought about Carl and what happened and their messed-up life together. Then it spilled out over everything.

"What about Bob?" Maryanne didn't clarify the question.

Bob Andrews, Carl's silent business partner. Silent even to her when they first launched the business. Another one of Carl's secrets that he'd justified as a necessary business decision. Despite her protests, Bob also acted as their financial planner. He was the one who was supposed to be watching over the business and family investments and debts. The first one who showed up on Lauren's doorstep with his hand out, asking for a loan repayment after Carl disappeared.

Lauren couldn't think about Bob, one of Carl's oldest friends, without getting hit with a rage-induced headache. She'd never liked him. He was too slick. Talked too big. He'd always struck her as a blowhard. She and Carl had so many fights over Bob. "What about him?"

"Bob knew." Maryanne looked from Kayla to Lauren. "About Carl's plans to leave. At least that's what Carl said. He owed Bob and Jake money because of . . . you. Well, that's what he said. With him dead, they were supposed to be able to collect on a separate business insurance policy Bob took out on Carl as part of them being partners or something."

A wave of dizziness hit Lauren. She was grateful she was sitting down. It was also a good thing she hadn't eaten anything today because if she had she might just lose it.

So much deception. So many lies. It was as if every

man she knew thrived on messing with her. All but Garrett.

She ran through the other information Maryanne had dropped. Bob was Carl's original silent business partner. The same guy who tried to collect on an insurance policy and called in the loans on the business, plunging her deeper into debt after Carl first left. Lauren hadn't seen him or heard anything about him in more than a year. That wasn't nearly long enough for her taste. He was smarmy and a liar . . . and apparently so was Jake.

"Why are you really here, Maryanne?" Lauren still didn't get that part. If the plan was to hurt her, it wasn't working. She just didn't feel enough for Carl for that to happen. That lingering sense of nostalgia for the past and sadness for what happened to him was all she could muster. Those were enough to push her to want to solve his murder, but that's all she owed him now.

"I just needed . . ." Maryanne inhaled again, looking paler by the second. "I think I needed to see you. To take some sort of responsibility for hurting you."

Kayla frowned. "Have you done that yet?"

"Kayla." Lauren sent her friend the warning before looking at the younger woman again. They both knew what it was like to be screwed by Carl, though she doubted Maryanne understood the depth of the deception and how much Carl had used her when he swept her away on that boat and pretended to disappear. "Have you talked with the police about Bob?"

Maryanne shook her head. "Not yet."

"Do it." Lauren swallowed back the hard lump clogging her throat. "If you really want to do something for me, do that."

Maryanne hesitated a few seconds then practically ran out of the office. The second the younger woman left, all of the energy ran out of Lauren. She slumped back in her chair as her muscles shook.

Concern filled Kayla's eyes. "Are you okay?"

"I will be."

"You don't feel sorry for her, do you?"

Damn but she did. A little anyway. "Don't you?"

Chapter Six

GARRETT HUNG UP the phone from the briefing with Wren and Matthias as soon as Lauren walked in the door. Her cheeks were red from the wind and she rubbed her hands together despite the gloves. Christmas was coming fast, as was the snow. He'd hoped to be gone and in a cabin alone somewhere by the time both hit. He didn't see that happening now.

For the first time in years, he might not be alone on the anniversary of his parents' deaths. He had no idea what to think about that. He traditionally spent the day sitting, thinking, maybe listening to music. Nothing stressful. Not doing anything that made him think.

Helping Lauren, finding Carl's killer, would keep him busy. Detective Cryer made it clear there were a limited number of suspects—Lauren, Maryanne, Jake and Bob, the silent business partner. That was a tight pool and Garrett had already eliminated one of them. He needed to talk to her about the others so he could start putting the pieces together.

Once he collected the information he'd pore over the records. Debate scenarios with the detective, Lauren and Matthias. Run through everything, then do it again. He negotiated for a living. He assessed and analyzed. He vowed to put all of those skills to work for her, no matter how long it took.

He watched her peel off her winter coat and the bulky zip-up sweater she had on underneath. By the time she was done stripping out of her winter layers, he was sweating and she wore a white oxford shirt and faded jeans. The woman looked better in old jeans than most women he'd seen did in expensive ball gowns.

She was so comfortable with who she was. He never appreciated how sexy that was until he met her. She might be mysterious and private but she held herself with a certain confidence that said she could handle anything, including kicking a little ass.

Then he really looked at her. Saw the strain on her face. He knew why it was there but he asked anyway, giving her a chance to get it out. "You okay?"

She treated him to a small smile as she plopped down on the couch next to him. "Kayla told you."

"Technically Kayla told Matthias, who called me." Garrett was pretty sure they all knew how to send a group text but no one seemed to be using the skill. "Apparently we're in seventh grade. Next thing we'll be passing notes at recess."

She stretched her arm along the back of the sofa until her fingers just grazed his shoulder. "I'm not sure you still get recess in seventh grade."

He was dying to lift her, put her on his lap and take that shirt off. Seeing her was all it took. Hell, when she walked across a room his body flipped to launch mode.

He fought to keep his voice steady. "Don't ruin my bad analogy."

This time she really touched him. Her fingertips skimmed his arm. "She was pathetic, Garrett."

He could hear the concern in her voice. In her place he'd be celebrating, enjoying the fact that the other woman in his marriage had gotten dumped. Not her. No, Lauren was decent and kind. Tough on the outside but loving inside.

That's what attracted him at first. Her loyalty to Kayla. How hard she worked and the sound of her laugh.

Damn, he had it bad for her.

Which was why he was so desperate to protect her. She may not want it, but he planned to help anyway. "Is it possible she was playing you?"

She shrugged. "I guess."

She didn't sound convinced, so he tried again. Nudged a little harder this time. "She did run off with your husband and what little money you had."

"She didn't exactly win anything with that move."

He let out the breath he didn't even know he was holding. Every time he mentioned Carl he waited for a look of pain to shoot across her face. For any sign that she cared for him or still loved him. He couldn't spot any.

"True, but being left behind or tossed aside, or whatever happened, might have made her angry enough to kill him."

Lauren frowned at him. "She could barely finish a sentence."

The woman had been conned and still thought people were basically honest. He had no idea where that bone-deep belief came from. He sure didn't share it. He'd seen the worst in humanity. Watched people destroy each other over things that didn't matter. He hoped she never knew that truth.

"Last I checked finishing a sentence wasn't a requirement for killing." Not that he'd ever seen. "Revenge, money, love . . . those are three of the top reasons."

She continued to toy with his sweater, twisting it in her fingers then smoothing it out again. "Maybe."

"I love that you want to see the best in her."

She snorted. "It's not that. Don't make me out to be a saint."

He found her to be pretty human. That was the point. Flawed and compelling and just secretive enough to have him wanting to dig for more. "Okay, then what is it?"

"I know what it's like to be a victim of Carl Gallagher."

He refused to let her wear that tag. Shifting on the cushion, he faced her head-on. "You are not a victim."

"What am I?"

"A survivor." His fingertips trailed over her cheek and down to her chin. "A really sexy survivor."

"Are you making a pass?" She smiled as she said the words.

He totally was even though he'd promised he'd give her space. He'd never said it out loud but he'd thought it . . . and now he wanted to break that vow. "Would it work?"

She scooted a little closer to him, closing the distance without saying a word. "I thought we established you have a green light."

"That wasn't a temporary thing?" *Please say no.*

"No."

He could barely hear over the buzzing in his ears. "Be sure, Lauren."

She didn't hide her movements this time. She slid across the couch, or tried to. When that didn't work, she lifted up on one knee and threw her other leg across his lap until she straddled him. Right there on the couch.

"You are the one thing I am sure of." She dipped her head and treated him to a very sweet lingering kiss.

He wanted more and that scared the hell out of him. Not enough to stop, but a warning sign did flash in his brain for a second before he blinked it out. "Those are big words."

"I know." She slid her hands around his neck. "What are you going to do about them?"

The woman wanted a gesture? Fine, he'd give her one.

With both hands cupped under her ass, he found his balance and stood up. Took her with him and had to smile when she wrapped her legs around his waist.

Her eyebrow lifted. "Impressive."

"I can only do that once a year. Don't get used to the move."

"Noted."

Her smile nearly knocked him out. Warmth and longing thrummed off her. He could feel her need, her excitement. It ran through her and vibrated against him.

He spun around, dropping them both on the mattress. She fell back and he balanced on top of her. They were fully dressed but he could feel every curve through their clothes. The scent he associated with her, the smell of fresh linen and a touch of flowers he could not name. He knew it came from her shampoo because he'd smelled it in the bathroom this morning after her shower. It had followed him around all day, baiting him.

His fingers went to the small white buttons on her shirt. One by one he opened them, revealing inch after inch of bare skin. He skimmed his fingers over her neck and across her collarbone. Trailed them down her chest to the tops of her breasts.

"You are so beautiful."

"And you are charming." She tugged on his sweater,

lifting it up his back. "Hot and charming with the touch of the devil inside you, I think."

That worked for him. The sweater didn't. His skin was on fire and everywhere she touched came alive under her hand.

She pushed up just enough to give him some room. He nearly ripped his sweater and tee to shreds getting them off. He wanted to strip it all off, but he slowed down. Just enough to savor her. To watch as her pupils dilated and her tongue darted out to wet her bottom lip.

She was sexy without even trying.

Then her hands were on him. Trailing over his shoulders and down his arms. Skipping to his chest and traveling over his stomach. Every brush, every touch, had his breath hitching inside him.

He kissed her then and tried to figure out why he hadn't done it the minute she walked in the door. Their mouths met and his mind went blank. All thought dropped out of his head except for his need for her.

Their bodies rubbed together as he shifted, working his fingers to get her shirt open and off. Tugging the material as he kissed her. Slipping his hand inside the silky laciness of her bra and loving the feel of her soft skin under his palm.

She gulped in a breath as he touched her. Her hands rested against the pillow near her head and her legs fell open. It was a surrender of sorts and he didn't squander the opportunity. His mouth slipped to her neck then traveled lower. He savored every taste of skin as he nosed her bra to the side and slipped her nipple into his mouth.

She groaned then. Her back arched off the bed. He opened his eyes just long enough to watch her stretch, to see her head fall back, exposing her neck. He wanted to lick every inch of her and vowed to do just that. He would take however long she gave him. And when her hand snaked down between them to find the zipper of his pants, he would have given her just about anything she wanted.

His mouth slid over her, caressing first one breast then the other with his tongue. As his lips worked, his fingers slipped to her jeans. Their hands knocked together as they yanked on zippers and pushed their pants down to the tops of their hips.

She brushed the back of her hand over him through his pants. Once . . . twice . . . until his lower body jerked in response.

"Jesus, Lauren." He could hear the pleading in his voice and didn't try to disguise it.

"Get the rest of your clothes off." She glanced down. "And mine."

"Yes, ma'am."

He loved that she knew what she wanted. There was no hiding her body—or her needs—from him. In the past she'd insisted being six years older than him was a problem, but he was only seeing the benefits.

He stretched up and kissed her again. Their mouths met and she made this soft humming sound. The noise burned through the last of his control. He was almost frantic to get her naked now. He reached behind her and unhooked her bra. Lifted her back off the mattress and stripped the shirt and bra off, leaving her open to his gaze. And he did not wait. His hands skimmed over her and his mouth followed. He licked and sucked until she called out his name. He had never heard anything sexier.

He moved then, slipping down and down. Pulling off her jeans and the tiny pair of white bikini underwear underneath. Sitting up he slipped off her boots and let them thud against the floor. A few yanks and everything was off. Every last stitch of material.

His body screamed for him to grab a condom and slide over her, but she stopped him. Not with words or a hand. No, she shifted her legs, bringing them up until her feet rested flat against the mattress. Then she let her thighs drop open wide.

The move was so sensual, so inviting, that he heard the screeching in his brain as his mind shut off and his body took over. Those lean legs and defined muscles. The tiny strip of hair that covered her.

Fucking damn.

He lowered his head and breathed in, taking in the scent of her. Brushing his lips lightly over the sensitive skin of her inner thighs. Hearing her long, drawn-out moan. Then his mouth was on her, his tongue inside her. He licked as he opened her. Kept at it with his finger and his tongue until her hips bucked and her mouth dropped up.

Looking up the length of her he saw nothing but a beautiful, amazing woman totally in control of her body and handing off her pleasure to him. He happily took over the task. Pushing her legs toward her chest, he opened her even further and saw her suck in a gulp of air in response.

"Garrett, please."

That's all it took. That husky voice and the final okay. He practically bounced up from the bed and stripped the rest of his clothes off. His belt flew here and his pants landed over there. He stopped only long enough to think about where he'd stashed the condoms.

The answer hit him fast and hard. The drawer next to the bedside. He'd thrown some in there while she was in the shower. Hopeful thinking and all that. The wooden drawer creaked as he ripped it open and grabbed a packet. Then he came back to her, slid over her, gasping at the friction of her body against his.

The room heated and the sound of their breathing filled the air. The mattress gave under their joint weight, plowing her head deeper into the pillows. She didn't complain and he didn't stop. He slid into the space between her open thighs and kissed her again. Slipping his tongue against hers, tangling his fingers in her hair.

He was riding the edge. His control held, but only by a thin tether. So when she dropped her hand, dragging her fingers over his bare chest and continuing lower, he stopped breathing. He couldn't even feel his heartbeat as she wrapped her hand around his length and pulled. She tightened her fingers and smoothed her hand up and down. The sensation mesmerized him. Had everything inside him tightening and begging for more.

But he wanted to end this time inside her. Condom on, head tipped back and hopefully with her screaming his name. At least that's the fantasy that played in his head. When he rolled the condom on and pulled her hand away, he knew he hovered right there, so close.

The months of foreplay and wanting had piled up. Touching her was enough to set him off. When he slipped inside her, just enough to feel her inner muscles clamp down on him, he broke out in a sweat. It gathered on his shoulders and across his back.

He tightened his muscles and tried to hold off the final moment for as long as possible, to savor every first with her. He might have succeeded if she hadn't moved. One lift of her hips, one trail of her tongue down his neck, and he was fucking done.

He plunged inside her, going slow and deep on the first thrust as she wrapped her body around his. Her breath echoed in his ear and her fingernails scraped across his bare shoulders. He could feel her, taste her and smell her. There wasn't a part of him that didn't touch her. And when he started to move, pulling in and out, mixing the rhythm and pressing his hips forward with every pass, her fingers slipped into his hair.

She pulled his head close. The sounds of her harsh panting matched his as she leaned up to whisper in his ear. "Faster."

"Fuck yes."

He lost it then. All control abandoned him and he rode her. Forget finesse and taking it slow. She didn't hold back and neither did he. Not now that he was inside her, surrounded by her warmth.

His orgasm hovered right there on the fringes but he wanted her with him. His hand went to the juncture of her legs and his finger slipped over her, hit that spot. He knew when it happened because she gasped and a resurgence of heat moved into her eyes. Then she was bucking, her hips tightening around him. He could feel the orgasm hit her and he let his body follow hers.

Instinct took over. He couldn't tell how or when they finished. All he remembered was the sound of a rough breath sneaking out of her throat and the insistent pounding of his heart. It thumped loud enough to block out every other noise.

With his body emptied and her lying in a satisfied sprawl beneath him, he finally let his head drop. His forehead touched hers as he fought to regain his strength, his breathing—something.

After a few minutes of comfortable silence, she unwrapped her legs from around his hips and let them fall on the mattress on either side of him. Her fingers massaged the back of his neck as they balanced there together.

"That was as great as I thought it would be."

His eyes popped open and he lifted his head to stare down at her. "You dreamed about us doing this?"

A sexy smile crossed her lips. "All the time."

"Then what the hell have we been waiting for?" He almost yelled the question. He'd been so hot for her, so careful but so ready.

Her fingers tightened against his skin as she held him close. "I had to be sure."

He wasn't quite clear on what that meant, but it didn't sound bad. "Are you sure now?"

"Definitely."

He let that be good enough. For today. He'd negotiate for more later.

Chapter Seven

HER BODY STILL tingled the next day. Once they had sex, they didn't stop having it. Lauren's thighs ached in the most delicious way. She hadn't experienced that feeling—the puffy lips, the sensitive breasts, that sensation of being filled—in so long.

Even before Carl left, he had checked out of their marriage and moved into the extra bedroom. Since she was never quite sure about his commitment to either fidelity or her, she hadn't fought the move to the extra bedroom. She handled what she needed herself. Tricked her brain and body into thinking that was enough for her. But the truth was she loved being touched and being with someone who appreciated her body and took care of it. She'd missed the sounds a man made when she wrapped her fingers around him. Now, thanks to Garrett, it all came rushing back.

He was as good as she'd known he'd be. Not selfish. Almost worshipping when it came to her nearly thirty-seven-year-old body. She was in good shape, but gravity was gravity and he didn't seem to notice. She thanked the universe for his failing eyesight or whatever it was that had him kissing and licking her, running his hands over her, as if she was a tight twenty-something.

"Uh, Lauren?"

Lost in her own thoughts, it took a minute for the words to break through. She looked up to see Garrett's knowing smile and realized he was the one who'd cleared his voice and called her name.

"Sorry." But she wasn't. Not for the night before. Not for this morning. Her only regret was agreeing to this meeting.

At just past ten, she sat with Garrett, Jake and Bob around the small table in the corner of her office. She'd pushed the business pamphlets and paperwork to the side to make room for everyone, though Matthias still stood at the door, keeping watch. The man looked ready to pounce, but she was pretty sure that was his usual look. Only Garrett seemed calm. Maybe repeated sex did that to a guy.

Bob leaned across the table, focusing only on her. "What did Carl say to you when he came back into town?"

She'd been asked that question so many times that she started to doubt how innocuous Carl's stop at her door really was. This time Bob demanded to know, as if he had a right to ask her for anything. She'd been furious with Carl over his screwed-up financial dealings and all the lies. How he actually went to the extra step to falsify documents just to throw her off. Who did that sort of thing?

But the simmering rage for Carl's antics didn't compare to what she felt for Bob. She despised Bob, the self-proclaimed financial guy who gave Carl investing and business advice. He pretended to be an innocent victim to Carl's scams, but she didn't buy it.

"Carl didn't say anything. Literally nothing of any interest." That wasn't a lie. Other than ticking her off, Carl's comments had been unremarkable, which was saying something since he'd just risen form the dead.

Bob's eyes narrowed. "Tell us exactly. Line for line."

"She walked through this with me and again with Matthias. Another time with the police and Detective Cryer." Garrett leaned back in his chair. "That's probably enough of that unless you have a specific question for her about a specific topic."

Bob's frown only deepened. "Who are you two again?"

"I'm an interested party," Matthias broke in and then nodded in Garrett's direction. "He's Lauren's boyfriend."

She waited for a *not exactly* or something similar from Garrett, but he stayed quiet. Only Jake shifted in his chair. "Since when?"

"It's recent," Garrett said.

Sure, now he piped up. She fought off the urge to roll her eyes.

"Carl came to *my* house and asked to come in." She made sure to emphasize the *my* part. "He wanted to pick up where he left off and wasn't offering any explanations, even though I asked for them. He was there all of ten minutes before he left."

"And then came back and was killed." Bob wore a self-satisfied grin. At forty, his hair had started to recede and his shiny good looks had faded a bit, but he still possessed that successful-and-flaunting-it air that many men of a certain age in the metro area had. The sharp navy suit. The matching unnecessarily expensive watch and sedan. And every now and then he dropped the name of the school he graduated from, as if anyone cared.

"Yes, Bob. We all know what happened." She kept her voice flat, hoping to telegraph just how done she was with Bob and his prepackaged persona.

"Do we?" Bob's gaze flipped between Garrett and Lauren. "You guys start going out, the husband comes back and now he's dead. Seems convenient, or maybe I should say inconvenient for you."

Garrett shifted just an inch and all the attention at the table flicked to him. "Do you have a question, Bob?"

That low steely voice suggested Bob should rethink this topic. The I-could-kick-your-ass tone had her mind drifting back to Garrett's comments about killing. He possessed an interesting mix of an easygoing charm and a commanding personality. He clearly was success-ful but never needed to spell that out for people. She could see it in his sure confidence. In the way he held his body and spoke. But underneath she wondered if maybe there was something a little bit lethal about him.

"It's suspicious." Bob opened his mouth as if he was going to say more, but one look at Garrett and he stopped.

Matthias finally pushed away from the wall and stepped toward the table. He didn't sit down. No, he stood, looming over Bob. "As suspicious as your know-ing Carl planned to fake his death so you could collect money from Lauren here and from a top-secret busi-ness insurance policy that you, not his wife, benefitted from?"

Bob snorted. "You obviously don't understand how this works. Business policies are routine."

So routine that no one bothered to talk to her about it. That fact kept spinning around in Lauren's head. The more she learned, the more she felt like she let her mar-riage happen to her rather than being an active par-ticipant. She had never been weak but when it came to Carl and their marriage she quickly ran out of energy and enthusiasm. She should have walked early on but stayed because everything she'd ever known about family had been skewed. She'd convinced herself that being with Carl was better than being alone. And she was wrong.

"Do you really want to have an argument with me

about how businesses operate?" Matthias leaned in closer to Bob. "Please say yes."

"And the part about you being in on the lie about Carl's death?" Garrett asked.

"That's a fucking lie." Bob looked from Garrett then up at Matthias. "It is."

She was more convinced than ever that Maryanne had told the truth, at least on that point. "Maryanne confirmed it."

"The chick Carl ran away with?" Bob snorted. "She's a—"

"Careful." Lauren knew some insulting word was going to come out of his stupid mouth and she shut that down. She hated that argument trick. The game where people went after a woman's looks or sexual activity to score points. It was derailing and insulting. Neither of those things were Bob's business and neither had any relationship to Maryanne's ability to tell the truth about the fraud.

Bob made an odd choking sound. "What, she's your friend now?"

"You can describe her, talk about her, without calling her names." That was Lauren's one rule. She likely had others, but she absolutely lived by that one.

Garrett winked at her. "Nice."

"Wait." Jake held up both hands. "I don't understand what's going on."

"Bob knew Carl planned to leave, knew he planned to engage in fraud." Matthias kept his arms crossed in front of him and he launched into the explanation. "Maryanne knew and likely would have stayed with Carl, but he dumped her. Because clearly that's his MO. He uses a woman and moves on. Maybe Maryanne got too old for him. Who knows."

The chair scraped against the weathered hardwood floor as Bob pushed it back and stood up. His furious scowl never left her. "And someone killed him in your locked house on your floor."

"Just say it, Bob." She dared him to call her a name this time. Garrett would likely jump across the table at him, but she'd bet she'd get there first.

But Bob didn't go there. "No one would blame you. He treated you like crap. He deserved it."

"Then why did you help him to disappear?" Garrett asked in a deadly cold voice.

"Never happened. That woman is lying."

Garrett shook his head. "We'll be able to trace the paperwork. Now that we know where to look, it's only a matter of time."

"There is nothing to find." He stepped away from the table and around Matthias, who hadn't moved an inch to get out of the way. "And I'm done here."

Bob stormed out without a glance. He'd fallen back on his anger. Lauren had looked for signs of something else—guilt or fear—but saw nothing. His nerves either ran ice-cold or Maryanne had spun a believable tale and Lauren got trapped in it.

The door still shook from the force of Bob's slamming it. No one else in the room moved. Boats bobbed in the marina and the constant clanking of boat lines and metal provided the only sounds around them.

It was another few seconds before Garrett spoke up. "That went well."

His voice seemed to snap Jake out of whatever haze he'd fallen into. He glanced at Lauren. "May I talk with you for a second? Outside."

When Garrett started to get up, she gestured for him to sit again. She could handle this. Hell, she wanted to handle this. Her life kept spinning around her, preventing her from moving forward. It was time for her to take back control, and that started right now.

GARRETT WATCHED JAKE and Lauren go. He didn't like her wandering out of his sight. Not that he didn't trust her. He did. She was smart and could handle herself, but Garrett knew that sometimes mere seconds were the difference between a rescue and a horror.

"Sounds like Lauren believes Maryanne. Do you?" Matthias pulled out the chair Jake just left and sat down. As was his practice, he wore an outward calm while he constantly scanned the area for threats.

Matthias lived his whole life that way. The man was paranoid, but with good reason. He ran a security company that supplied forces to everyone from wealthy businessmen to political leaders. He'd seen shit that was even worse than Garrett had experienced during his black ops days, and that was saying something.

"Not really, but I'm not sure I trust many people." Garrett ignored how hardass that sounded and continued his thought. "Maryanne had a reason to want Carl dead—revenge, jilted lover and who knows what he did to her while they were away. Bob clearly was in on all of this and might have killed Carl to cover his tracks. And Jake."

Matthias's eyebrow lifted. "What about him?"

"Unrequited love."

"Excuse me?"

"He has a thing for Lauren." Garrett didn't find the sentiment any less punch-worthy now than he had before.

Matthias glanced out the window then back to Garrett. "For his sister-in-law? That's creepy as fuck."

"I don't know how to say it without sounding creepy." There really was no way to pretty it up. "But I'm not sure Lauren sees it."

Matthias shook his head. "I wish I could unsee it."

"Then we have the problem of the locks and the alarms. Lots of motives, but how did the killer get in?" When Matthias started to talk, Garrett spoke right over him. "And do not tell me the evidence points toward Lauren."

Matthias took another look outside. This time his gaze lingered a bit longer before he responded. "Oh, please. No way did she do it."

The concentration break didn't bother Garrett. He guessed Matthias was keeping a watchful eye on Lauren outside. So long as that was true, Matthias could do all the staring he wanted to. But the emphatic support of her was still a surprise because Matthias suspected everyone. "Look at you, believing in people. That's new."

"First, Kayla loves her so even if Lauren did kill the fucker, and I totally would get why because that guy was an ass wipe, I'd support her. I'd also give her a lecture on better ways to hide the evidence."

"I love your practical side." Only Matthias. Actually, no. Most of the Quint Five would answer that way. Since he'd started hanging out with them and spending most of his days with Wren, the response made sense to Garrett. He ran with a very protect-your-own crowd.

"Pissing off Kayla does nothing for my private life." Matthias shot Garrett a man-to-man you-get-me look. "Besides, I don't see how Lauren, a woman who is sympathetic to her husband's mistress, is a killer. It doesn't fit."

Garrett both loved and hated Lauren's quick support of Maryanne. Name calling was bullshit and Bob had deserved to be censored before he could malign her. But having Lauren believe in Maryanne worried him because the other woman might be cut from the same con-artist cloth as Carl. She just might be better at scamming, and Lauren had been through enough.

"My money is on Bob. If he was in on the drowning, I'm betting he helped fake the bank and investment documents that fooled Lauren, too." Matthias took a bottle of water from the center of the table and cracked open the lid. "Have you seen them? Wren says they are expert quality, which makes me wonder if Bob is pulling a scam on anyone else."

"Well, I've read the file Wren compiled on Carl. He wasn't the brains here. Lauren kept the place afloat despite him then thrived once his inept management was gone."

"Bob is a financial guy. If people find out he's playing with documents and running frauds, he loses everything." That sounded like motive to Garrett.

"And if Carl didn't stay dead as planned, he made himself into a loose end."

"Exactly."

"I'll have Wren dig deeper." Matthias took another look out the window. "In the meantime, you may want to head outside. The conversation between Lauren and her lovesick brother-in-law looks serious." Matthias shook his head. "The creepy fucker."

At least Garrett wasn't the only one saying it now. "That's exactly how I think of him."

JAKE STOOD IN front of Lauren on the pier. The smell of fish and salt and dampness floated around them. Boats rested in the water next to them and her back stayed to the office. She knew if she looked in the window and saw Garrett peeking out she'd have to roll her eyes, and that couldn't happen. Not when Jake seemed very serious.

The color had drained from his face. "Boyfriend?"

"That's the part that bothers you?" They'd talked about fraud and Carl's games. Bob's possible complicity. And Jake was worried about her love life, something she hadn't had until very recently.

"I've seen him around. Heard rumors."

About Garrett? That didn't make sense. "What?"

Jake folded his arms across his stomach and stopped shifting around. His intense gaze never wavered. It stayed trained on Lauren. "I had no idea you guys had moved to the serious stage."

Apparently she was supposed to make some sort of public announcement. That was news to her, so was the idea of having a boyfriend.

Rather than fight Jake on this and get frustrated, she went with standard relationship lingo. In this case, it fit. "It's complicated."

"Look, Lauren." Jake's arms dropped to his sides and he moved in closer. "I don't want to see you get hurt. How much do you know about this guy?"

Right before he could take her hand, she stepped back. Jake had always been the touchy type. At first she thought it was sweet. As someone with no real family, being enveloped by Carl's comforted her like the perfect soft blanket. But then it got weird.

Jake had turned strangely possessive after Carl disappeared. She knew it was his way of protecting her, but the last thing she wanted was to spend time with anyone related to Carl. Unfortunately, that included Jake, which she knew wasn't fair, but nothing about her marriage and interpersonal relationships was.

She tried to turn the conversation back to the real reason they'd met today. Sure, it was for Matthias and Garrett, with Detective Cryer's blessing, to size up two of the other suspects. But she really did want answers. "Look, the bigger issue here is Carl and finding his killer."

"Bob." Jake sighed. "I hate to say it but he has the most to lose."

"How did he get into my house?" That was the piece she couldn't make fit in her head. The lack of a break-in suggested someone close enough to be able to come and go. The only person who fit that description was Kayla.

"He's connected. He probably could have had keys made. I think—"

Garrett stepped onto the pier and walked over to him. He didn't bother closing the door to the office behind him. "Everything okay out here?"

"We were talking about keys." She smiled as she said the words, but something tickled in the back of her mind. A memory she couldn't grab on to.

Garrett made that familiar humming sound that he usually made before he made a smartass comment. "I'd say 'That's interesting' but it really isn't."

Jake's eyes narrowed as he watched Garrett. "Can you give us a few more minutes?"

"No." No reason. Garrett just denied the request and stood there.

The response had Jake blinking. "Excuse me?"

"Lauren and I have a meeting with the detective."

"Oh, right." Never mind that it was news to her. She used it as the excuse to start heading for the office. She hesitated just long enough to call to Jake over her shoulder. "I'll call you."

"You do that."

She waited until Jake was out of earshot. "Do we really have a meeting with the detective or were you being a jerk to Jake for fun?"

Garrett finally broke eye contact with Jake's retreating back. "I don't like anyone in that family but you."

Something about that statement sent a shiver racing through her. "I'm not in it anymore."

"Anyone else lurking around? His parents or a stray cousin?"

"No. His parents were older. They died in the first few years we were married. One right after the other." She remembered mourning them. They'd raised two very different sons. Carl, outgoing and flirtatious with a mean streak. Jake, handsome but quiet, pretty unassuming.

"That doesn't really help the case."

Then the memory clicked. The keys. That was it.

She held up a finger as she headed for the office. "I think I have something that might."

"Clue me in . . ." His voice trailed off. "Where are you going?"

She stepped back inside. Didn't even stop when Matthias looked up from studying one of her business pamphlets. She slipped behind her desk and pushed her chair to the side. There, under the drawer was an open space. She reached in and pulled out a set of keys. Held them up by the far edge and let them jangle in her hand.

"Huh." Garrett stared at her. "I feel like I should be more excited about this reveal."

The man really knew how to kill a big moment. "My extra set of keys."

"To your house." Garrett said it more as a statement than a question.

Excitement ran through her. This could explain so much. "The house. This office, which is unlocked all day while I'm in and out. And to the boathouse up the pier."

"You think someone came in and took them," Matthias said in a flat tone that mirrored the one Garrett now used.

She had no idea what was wrong, so she kept talking. One of them would clue her in eventually. "It wouldn't be that hard. I don't use them every day. I wouldn't notice if they were gone."

Matthias made a baggie appear out of nowhere. "Drop them inside. It's unlikely since there were no prints in your house, but there could be on these."

"That doesn't explain the alarm," Garrett said as he watched Matthias handle potential evidence.

This is where the explanation got a little tricky. "Human error."

Her brain had been wrapped in a haze that afternoon. She'd texted Garrett, which secretly thrilled her, but the shock of Carl's sudden disappearance hadn't worn off. No matter how hard she tried, she couldn't remember each step she'd taken when she walked out of the house that day.

Garrett froze. "What?"

"I don't always turn it on."

"Why have the damn thing?" All emotion left Garrett's face, but he could yell. Boy, could he yell.

"I was with you and . . ." *Well, crap.* When both men continued to look at her as if she needed a reality check, she finished the thought. "I felt safe."

Garrett shook his head. "You're killing me here."

She didn't think he meant it in the sexy way. She got the distinct impression he was struggling to hold on to his temper.

Matthias shot Garrett a quick glance before looking at her again. "At least we have a possible way for someone to get in that doesn't incriminate you."

The room started to spin. The dizziness hit her out of nowhere and she grabbed for the chair to keep from falling over. "Is that an issue?"

"Your house. Your dead husband."

Matthias did like to boil things down to their essence. Right now she would have preferred a little tact. "When you put it that way . . ."

"It kind of reinforces the need to use that alarm,

doesn't it?" Garrett added a sigh at the end, as if she needed further confirmation that he was ticked off.

Message received. The painful gut-kicking part of this was she didn't know why Carl had snuck back to her house or who had followed him. But if she'd turned on the alarm, it was possible neither of them could have gotten in. Carl might still be alive.

That truth brought a whole new wave of guilt crashing into her. "It does now."

Chapter Eight

LAUREN THREW HER head back, desperate to drag air into her lungs. The warmth of the hotel room closed around her. Heat thrummed off Garrett's slick body underneath her. The mattress dipped where her knees dug in next to his hips.

She loved this position. On top of him. Surrounding him. Hands on his chest and staring down into that intense gaze.

Temptation pulled at her. Right then she wanted that mouth. It had been all over her. Licking and tasting, sometimes nibbling before kissing her sensitive skin again. She leaned down and his length pushed up inside her. The move had her gasping as her mouth closed over his. She breathed him in, taking his air as his hands smoothed over her breasts and around to her lower back.

He broke the kiss by tipping his head deep into the pillows. "You're killing me."

That was on purpose. The first time tonight had been fast. They'd walked in and he threw her on the bed. Stripped her and put her on her hands and knees. She'd never come so hard or so fast. But this time was for her. He told her to lead, to take control. And she loved the rush of power.

"I want to savor this," she whispered.

He put his hands on either side of her face and pushed her hair back. Held it there. "You have more faith in my control than I do."

That wasn't true and she *really* loved that part. When his body had started to take over and his hips began to buck a few minutes ago, she'd lifted off him. Told him he didn't have her permission. Damn if he didn't grit his teeth and tell her to get moving.

Now she wanted to hold out, to prolong the sensual torture. To slowly lift and lower her body as he squirmed and begged.

She licked her bottom lip . . . just because. "I believe in you."

"Fuck." His arms fell back on the mattress on either side of his head. "Take pity on me, woman."

She trailed her fingernails down his chest. Over the tight muscles and along the sharp dips. "You are so sexy."

He groaned. Then he shifted. The move was subtle, just the lift of one hip, but that's all it took. The last of the air rushed out of her. She sank deeper over him until the tightening inside her let go.

She rested her palms against his chest, felt his fingers brush over her arms and leaned in. Up and down. One last plunging fall and she lost it. The orgasm slammed into her. All that foreplay, all the touching, turned every inch of her into a sensitive quaking mess.

She could hear the noises in her throat as her head fell forward. Her back arched and her hair swept over her shoulder to hang in her face. With Garrett, she was free to be who she wanted and take what she needed. Without ever saying a word, he insisted she not hold back. With him she didn't.

When the final waves of pleasure moved through her, she inhaled nice and deep. Her body hummed as she lifted her head just enough to look at him. Their gazes met.

A hint of a smile played on his lips. "I could watch you do that every single day."

Before the words sank in, he wrapped an arm around her waist and flipped them over. Her back hit the mattress and on instinct her legs wrapped around him. The quick switch thrust him even deeper. Her skin and the tiny muscle inside her were already primed and sensitive. Having him rest there, pressing against her, was almost too much. Every breath he took echoed inside her.

"You okay?" He asked the question through rough breaths.

This man. In just a short time, and through all

her defenses, her feelings for him pushed past attraction. She actually liked him, wanted to be with him . . . dreaded the idea of him leaving to go back home.

She'd expended every ounce of energy but she found the strength to lift her hand. She skimmed her thumb over the stubble on his chin, across that sexy bottom lip, loving every angle. "I'm great. Thanks to you."

"I need—"

"Do it." She brought his head down for another heart-stopping kiss.

Her hands slipped over him. Across those shoulders and traveled down his back. And she kept going. Her palms stopped their tour on his firm ass and she cupped him in both hands.

He lifted his head and a sexy smile lit up his face. "Well, now."

"That was for me." She tightened her thighs against his hips. "Now tell me what you need."

"I have it." He started moving then. In and out of her, pushing and thrusting, scooping her into his arms.

He balanced his body over hers, rubbed against her until the heat blinded her again. Without another word, he buried his mouth in her neck. One last push and he blew out a long breath. His wet mouth touched her skin as his hips flexed and the orgasm tore through him.

His body rocked against her. The rumble in his chest vibrated against her as the last of the tension eased from him.

Opening her eyes, the hotel's white ceiling came

into focus. Her fingers played with the damp ends of his hair. The way he sprawled over her anchored her. She felt complete and satisfied and more than a little punch drunk from the whip of adrenaline that was only now dying down.

She'd suspected it would be like this with him. Right and a little abandoned. Totally free and accepting. Garrett was one of the few people she'd ever met who didn't disappoint her. He was exactly who he promised to be, beginning to end. She loved that about him.

The word floated through her mind and the exhaustion fled. No, not that. She'd been careful, even in her marriage, not to fall hard. She stayed in control, and that was certainly required with Garrett, the guy who held back as much as she did.

His past was a mix of memories and danger. None of that scared her. If anything, it reassured her that he could handle almost anything. For once, maybe she didn't have to be the adult. But this was fun.

Fun only. She repeated that mantra in her mind.

He lifted up and balanced his weight over her on his elbows. "What are you thinking about?"

The question caught her off guard. "What?"

"I can almost feel you thinking."

"That's not a thing." At least she hoped not.

He shifted to the side, easing out of her and taking some of his weight off her. "Honestly? You started making these strained noises. I think I could hear them because I was on top of you, but I'm guessing you weren't thinking about getting something to eat. Though I'm game, if you're wondering."

"May I ask you something?" She didn't have the right and she wasn't dying to know, but the more time they spent together the more she wanted to collect these pieces of him. Gather one here and one there until she had an image of the whole man in front of her. Not just what he wanted to show her, but who he really was. She knew from experience those could be two very different things.

He winced. "Experience tells me when someone asks for permission first, the question is going to carry a wallop, but go ahead."

"It's about the killing."

He rested his head on his palm and watched her. "Carl?"

"You."

"Wait." His hand dropped to his side. "What are we talking about?"

"You've hinted that . . . well, in your past . . ."

This time he shifted until he sat up, leaning against the pillows. "Are you asking if I've killed people?"

With the sheets wrapped around her, she eased up to sit next to him, careful not to touch him in case he didn't want to be touched. "I'm trying to figure out why you're familiar with killing."

"You are strangely calm about this topic."

She put her hand on his lap and sighed with relief when he slipped his fingers through hers. "I'm not afraid of you, if that's what you're trying not to ask."

"Why?"

"*Why?*" He continued to stare at her despite her stunned response, not showing any signs of explaining the question, so she tried another tact. "I've lived my entire adult life detached after spending every year before that as the only responsible one in my household."

His body came alive then. He didn't move, but energy pounded off him. He was interested and engaged. "What about your parents?"

"My dad was long gone by the time I could talk." That was the easy part. "My mom . . . uh . . ."

He squeezed her hand. "Would it be easier if you knew when I first met you I had a file on you?"

She shifted to face him. "Meaning?"

"It's part of what I do for Wren. I collect information." He brought their joined hands up to his mouth and placed a quick kiss on the back of hers. "I know your mom died when you were seventeen."

"Do you know the details?"

"I didn't look. Didn't think they were relevant."

She laughed but she there was no amusement in the sound or inside her. "Some people think my past explains why I am the way I am."

"Loving? Smart? Driven? Sexy as hell?"

"Aloof."

He shook his head. "I've told you before. That one doesn't fit."

"She battled depression and these incredible cycles where she moved and talked at hyperspeed. It was nonstop. No sleep. No eating. Just racing around and solving these puzzles that only seemed to exist in her head." More than a decade later the memories clicked into place. She didn't have to dig to find them. No, she'd spent years trying to smooth out the edges and file them away. "She hated the meds because they made everything dull and colorless."

"That's a lot to handle as a kid."

"That was easy compared to the times when nothing mattered and she wanted out." Lauren gulped in air but it did nothing to ease the lump in her throat. "She tried and failed, then one day she succeeded."

"She killed herself." Garrett cradled her hand in both of his now.

"Ran her car into a tree." Lauren rested her head against the wall and fought off a punch of grief. This one was new, fresh. A reminder that her job had always been to take care of other people. The only thing she learned was not to let her emotions engage, not get close enough to get sucked under again. "She was on the phone with me at the time."

He didn't say anything but he did move. His arm came around her, tucking her in close to his side. His thumb rubbed her shoulder and his lips brushed her hair. He enveloped her in a comforting hold that made her feel cherished and safe.

She'd tried to explain her upbringing to other people. Told them parts of the story and watched the pity overtake them. Heard every comment about her mother "being in a better place now" and how everyone had someone like that in their family. They all meant well, but the words and those lame phrases only caused her to shut down faster.

Garrett didn't try to make her feel better in the usual ways. The hug was so much more effective, so she closed her eyes and fell into him. For just a few minutes let her mind clear. Pushed out the list of things she needed to do and handle and worry about, and let the sound of his steady breathing guide her.

"The killings." For almost a minute that's all he said. "Before I worked for Wren I worked for the government. My official career was with the National Geospatial-Intelligence Agency."

She froze. She debated saying anything because she was desperate to hear him talk, to know more about what had shaped and created Garrett McGrath. "I don't even know what that is."

"It's about monitoring and assessing data and images and where people and military equipment are located and how they're shifting."

"Just say spy stuff."

He laughed. "That's a line losers give in bars to get sex."

"I can't imagine it works."

"Who knows? I've never tried it." He settled deeper

into the pillows as his body relaxed. "The point is I did do that work, but that's not really who I worked for."

She separated from him and sat up, letting the sheet dip in front of her but not caring. "Oh, my God. So, I was right. Actual spy stuff."

"I did black ops work, which I can't talk about and don't want to, but that's where I saw death. That and a mix of bad decisions, questionable management and unnecessary loss of innocents." He exhaled. "And you are the only one outside of a small group of friends— small as in five—that know that."

"I trust you, too." The words popped out but she meant them.

He cupped her cheek. "I lost my parents when I was a little older than you were. Just a kid, really. Every choice I made after that, including seeking out a career that I believed allowed me to know the unknowable, both at the agency and now, stems from the car accident that took them."

A chill ran through her. Their lives, so different on the surface, mirrored each other in some ways. Early deaths defined them and their decisions. Losing people they loved shoved them onto a path that made them responsible for others.

She understood him.

"If we were dating I'd say we just learned something important about each other." She tried to make a joke but the tone didn't come off right.

Tipping her mouth up, he kissed her. Slow and sweet

until the end when he treated her to that sexy tongue. He lifted his head again. "I agree—we definitely learned one important thing over the last few days."

Those eyes, that rough voice—she was mesmerized, hanging on his words. "What?"

"We *are* dating."

Chapter Nine

THE ALARM ON Garrett's watch sounded at two in the morning. He'd re-routed the new silent alarm at Lauren's house straight to his watch. Actually, Matthias had, but the result was the same. It got Garrett's attention.

He'd been on his side in bed, curled around Lauren's naked body, finally drifting off to sleep after hours of touching her. Now he was up and dressed. Freezing his balls off on the sidewalk in front of her house with Lauren at his side.

He really wanted to leave her back at the hotel, locked in and safe. She made it clear when she got dressed and threatened to kick him that she did not agree. "This could be dangerous."

She didn't look at him. Her focus stayed on her front porch. "More dangerous than those two guys walking around with guns while they try to fade into my shrubbery?"

The men, dressed in black and carrying, stalked the house. They moved around the grounds, without a sound and out of sight. They only popped into view when Garrett pulled up a few houses down. But they'd been on site since Carl's body was found, blending in and slipping into the darkness when needed.

"They work for Matthias."

She nodded as she tucked her hands in her jacket pockets. "That's oddly comforting."

Garrett agreed. Matthias only hired the most qualified. His teams were trained, serious and lethal. They obeyed orders and did not mess around. They also breached the house as soon as Garrett called to say the motion sensor went off but had no luck catching anyone.

One of the guards slipped around the house and in just a few steps stood in front of them. "We checked. No one is in there." He spoke to them but his gaze continuously scanned the area. "No obvious signs of anything being taken."

"How did anyone get around you?" Lauren's sounded fascinated, not accusatory.

"Not possible." The guard met Garrett's gaze and held it for a few seconds. "It's a false alarm."

Garrett did not want to get in the middle of a pissing match. He knew better than to go up against a guy carrying at least three weapons. And those were the ones he could see. Garrett was pretty sure there were more, but he didn't want to test the theory.

"Save that for your boss." He nodded at the guard then looked at Lauren. "Stay here."

"Not happening."

Garrett was pretty sure he saw the guard smile at her refusal but Garrett kept his full attention on her. "Lauren."

"You can say my name as many times as you want. The answer will be the same. No." She unzipped her jacket and headed for the front door.

"Don't smile. It only encourages her." Garrett mumbled the comment under his breath to the guard before reaching out and snagging Lauren's arm. "You stay behind me and don't touch anything."

"In my own house?"

He used the key he'd made to open the front door. "These comebacks. You really are on your game at two in the morning. I need to remember that for next time."

"I'm hoping this doesn't keep happening."

Garrett didn't respond because he didn't disagree. He slipped inside, careful not to disturb anything. He'd turned off the sensors to keep his watch and Wren's console back at his office from going haywire.

He glanced around the room. Didn't spy anything out of the ordinary. He remembered the layout of the floor and had studied the photographs enough times to know where and how Lauren kept everything, down to the box sitting next to the couch filled with Christmas ornaments.

He didn't need that reminder. Time ticked down to the holiday, Garrett's least favorite of the year. His only comfort came in slipping away in quiet each year. He'd been dodging decorations and holiday displays for months. Lauren hadn't put up a tree yet, but the box was clearly marked.

Walking around, he realized he couldn't hear anything. The room was silent. She'd stopped talking and her boots didn't sound on the floor. He whipped around to find her standing over the spot where Carl's body once rested. "Lauren?"

Her face was drawn and devoid of color when she glanced up at him. "The floor is clean."

He wasn't sure what to do here. Did he usher her out or put an arm around her? He honestly had no idea what the proper protocol was for this sort of thing. For his work cases, Wren had a team of people who came in and took care of the hand-holding.

After a few seconds of indecision, he went with talking. Nothing else. "I had a service handle it once Detective Cryer gave me the okay."

Her mouth twisted in a frown. "Someone had to see that?"

"It's a specialty company. They clean crime scenes." He could see her sharp intake of breath and took a step toward her.

Instead of breaking down or yelling—both would

have been understandable—she shook her head and inched back from the now invisible outline of blood. "That sounds like a terrible job."

"But necessary." He went to her this time. Rubbed his hands up and down her arms. "Anything obvious?"

She gave the area within view a quick look. "No. Could this have been a false alarm?"

Anything was possible but Garrett didn't believe in coincidences. "We set up motion sensors. Something set one of them off."

Her eyebrow lifted. "How did you manage that?"

That tone he recognized. She brought it out when dealing with business matters and when she thought he was trying to walk over her. It bugged him at first but now it was one of his favorite things about her. It meant Lauren was Lauren. She wasn't locked in the past or swept away by anger or grief.

"Carl came here for a reason, possibly to look for something since he waited until you weren't here to come in. If true, I thought the person who killed him might come back looking for the same thing."

"Whatever that was."

"Exactly." Garrett wasn't used to explaining his actions. Wren gave him a lot of room to maneuver. Garrett had worked Kayla's case with Matthias and had his trust as well. "There was a small chance, so I took it."

"Smart."

The tension pinging around the room died down. "Thanks."

She stepped into the kitchen and opened a few cabinets. "Any chance you set up cameras, too?"

He guessed there was a right answer to this. He knew what it was. He hoped she did. "Actually . . ."

Her head shot around and she looked at him again. "Really?"

"A few. I called Wren. He's checking the feed."

She treated him to a small smile. "You guys take this stuff seriously."

"Your being in danger? Yes, I do."

She started to say something but stopped when the front door opened. Matthias stepped in wearing a suit without a tie, further convincing Garrett the guy didn't own anything else.

"Hey." Matthias kept his hand on Kayla's elbow as he ushered her inside. "She insisted on joining me."

"Of course I did." Kayla glanced at Garrett. "But I couldn't convince him to wear the casual clothes I bought him."

Garrett winked at her. "Next time."

"What are we looking at here?" Matthias asked as he stepped further into the living area.

Lauren pulled a water bottle out of the refrigerator and motioned to the rest of the room. They all shook their heads and she kept it for herself. "Matthias, I don't understand how someone got around your guys and got in here."

Matthias smiled at Garrett. "You didn't tell her that part?"

Confusion spread across Lauren's face. "What?"

Garrett had figured this was part of the setup he and Matthias discussed. Now he had confirmation. "When you want to trap someone inside, you lure them in. You don't make it hard."

"Did you leave her door open?" Kayla asked.

"That would be a rookie move. Too obvious." Matthias shrugged. "Cracked two hard-to-reach windows in different locations in the house and someone took the bait."

Kayla leaned up and kissed Matthias on the cheek, not an easy feat since the guy was about six-four. "That's pretty hot."

Since Garrett would rather be anywhere but at the house that held all the bad memories for Lauren, he kickstarted the conversation. "We had an alarm in the bedroom and one in here. The place is clear of intruders but who knows what else we might find."

"We'll get started in the bedroom," Kayla said as she reached out for Lauren's hand. The two of them disappeared into the other room a second later.

Garrett headed for the front windows then crouched down to check the sensors. He expected Matthias to head for another part of the cottage but he loomed right there. It was enough to make Garrett stand up again. He knew something was coming.

"Having a good night?" Matthias asked from right behind Garrett.

He knew Matthias well enough to know the question

he asked was not really his question, and he braced for more. "Up until a half hour ago."

"Still just being a bodyguard? Doing bodyguard stuff?"

That didn't take long. Garrett had been expecting it but Matthias still landed the shot pretty well. "We can look without talking. I'm fine with that."

"Be careful."

The change in Matthias's tone had Garrett paying attention. "A warning? Really?"

For a guy who excelled at negotiating and strategizing, he seemed to be doing a pretty shitty job of maneuvering through his relationship with Lauren. He'd dated before. He had no idea why this was so different. So much bigger. Whatever it was, it made him careful with what he said.

"This time I'm worried about you, not her."

"I'm trying to believe we're having this conversation." Garrett would be happy to have it end anytime now. Really.

Matthias scoffed. "That makes two of us."

He took off for the kitchen at twice his normal speed. Garrett had to smile at that. Matthias was not a man known for running from anything. But Garrett still needed to make a point. "We're seeing if there's anything between us. Just . . . you know, seeing."

Matthias stilled. "Do you hear yourself?"

His stammering was tough to miss. Even Garrett had to admit that. "Unfortunately."

"You swoop into town—"

"Swoop?" Not a word Garrett ever remembered saying before.

"You might have just started sleeping together, which is the only explanation for that stupid look on your face, but you guys have been circling each other for months. Dating without dating."

Garrett was pretty sure that was more words than Matthias had said all last month. But he did say something worth noting. "I tried to tell Lauren about that dating part but she was in denial."

"Women." Matthias shrugged. "Look, I've never seen you like this before. With anyone. She might not be ready even if you are. Maybe go slow."

Garrett heard the tone. Not Matthias's usual grumbling bark. No, this was something different. "Is this warning from Kayla or from you?"

"I don't care about any of this." Matthias opened the refrigerator and took out something in a plastic container. He studied it but didn't open it. "You're consenting adults."

That was more like the Matthias he knew. But Garrett didn't buy it. Matthias wasn't the type to meddle. The uncomfortable talk was his way of saying he cared. That mattered to Garrett and he was close enough to Matthias to accept the advice without mentioning the emotion behind it.

He dropped the container back on the shelf and closed the door. "But, Garrett? Don't fuck this up.

You likely don't see it yet, but you guys make sense together."

That sounded like decent advice, so Garrett decided to take it. "Okay."

"And if you mess it up, Kayla will make me kill you."

LAUREN AND KAYLA walked around the office area in the bedroom. Stacks of unfiled paperwork teetered on the edge of her desk. This was her personal information, which she hadn't looked at or thought about but was pretty sure she was supposed to save. At work, everything was catalogued with bookkeeper perfection. Here she let things slide.

"You okay?" Kayla asked from the opposite side of the desk chair.

"I love that you keep asking that and expecting a different answer each time."

Kayla shrugged. "I guess I'm an optimist."

"What?" Lauren laughed. "You are not."

Kayla was incredible and loving, and she had a horrible past that made it hard for her to be anything other than practical and a bit wary. Things had changed a bit now that she was dating Matthias, but people didn't morph into something new. That was one thing Lauren was pretty clear about. Their general makeup, what mattered to them, stayed static.

"True, but back to Garrett . . ." Kayla cleared off an

edge of the desk and sat there, swinging her leg back and forth.

Dodge. That advice kept running through Lauren's head. She didn't know what she was doing with Garrett, so there was no way she could explain it.

"He's great." That sounded so ridiculous she immediately tried again. "I'm trying not to overanalyze."

Kayla's smile was a bit too happy. "What I've learned about Matthias and Garrett and their friends is that you don't need to overanalyze because they'll do it for you."

Lauren had no idea what that meant. "What?"

"If you don't think you're the main topic of conversation between them each day, you're wrong."

Lauren was pretty sure she swallowed her tongue. *"What?"*

Footsteps sounded in the hall, then Matthias and Garrett appeared in the doorway. One after the other, they stepped inside the room. With four adults, the furniture and all the files, it was claustrophobic.

"How are we doing up here?" Garrett asked as he moved to stand beside her.

"We have documents and . . ." Kayla grabbed a stack off the bookshelf. "And more documents. Then we have files and what look like old bank documents. Don't you get that stuff online like everyone else?"

"Wait." Lauren reached across the desk and Garrett's chest and grabbed the file. She held it tight to her as memories of the last thirty months ran through her head.

Garrett frowned at her. "You okay?"

A light clicked on inside her. She'd never experienced an aha moment before but now she knew the sensation. It spun through her.

She turned to Garrett and held the file out to him. "The documents. The bank statements. I've kept them."

Matthias looked around the desk. "It looks like you keep everything."

"No, you don't understand." She opened the file and passed it around for them to see. Showed them the top statement. "I realized the money mess Carl dragged us into when the creditors started calling. The police knew about the money issues and asked what felt like a million questions on the topic. But the bank statements, the fraud . . . I didn't share that with the police."

Kayla frowned. "What?"

"It's why I went to the divorce attorney right before Carl bolted. I asked questions and Carl wouldn't answer them, but I knew the statements didn't make any sense compared to how little money we had left over after expenses and Carl's credit cards." Lauren exhaled. "That lie was the one that broke me."

Kayla's head shot up. "But why hide this information from the police?"

"Because she didn't want to paint an even bigger target on her chest. She was already a suspect. Her husband cheats on her, runs up debts and lies to her then disappears." Garrett put a hand on her lower back.

"More evidence might have had the police looking in the wrong direction."

The tension buzzing in Lauren's head vanished as Garrett talked. He understood. He wasn't blaming her or judging. The expression on his face could only be described as pride. "And I needed Carl declared dead. I couldn't afford—literally—a protracted investigation or more lawyers."

"All those months of insisting he was dead." Kayla said the words slowly, as if the importance of them hit her as she spoke.

Lauren rushed to explain. "It was the only way to survive." She looked around the room, willing them all to understand. "Once I knew Carl scammed me I really didn't care where he was, but I was terrified of being blamed and not being able to defend myself."

Matthias nodded. "Smart."

"Very," Garrett said right after. "So we're dealing with someone who knows—"

"Bob." All the pieces slipped together then. She didn't know why she hadn't figured it out the second she saw Carl's body. She pointed to the business's name listed as a duplicate address for receiving the statements. "That's Bob's old company. It's changed its name, but it's him. He's a financial expert. How did he not know these weren't real? It was his job to manage our finances, to check."

Garrett searched through the file. "You said he was

the first one to come looking for a loan repayment when Carl disappeared."

"And he knew about the scam." Kayla sighed. "According to Maryanne."

"He might want to get his hands on these before you turn them over . . ." Garrett's voice trailed off then he lifted his head. "You are going to give these to the police this time, right?"

So few days had passed since they'd found the body. Detective Cryer had called and insisted they talk again. She needed to do it, but she'd barely had time to think. It was as if an endless parade of people filed in and out of her days. Police questions. Alarms. Garrett.

But she had to concentrate now. She needed her life back and the only way to take control was to grab it. "The police can have them. I actually didn't think about them until this second. I almost burned them last year."

Garrett looked at Matthias over the top of the file. "While we're burning things, I think we should ask to talk with Bob again."

"You can't kill him." Lauren tried to phrase it as a joke, but when no one laughed she was pretty sure she'd failed.

Garrett scoffed. "I'm not promising."

Chapter Ten

GARRETT REALLY WANTED to kill this guy. The only thing stopping him was Lauren. She made him promise this morning not to lose it. Then Wren made him promise to follow the rules and wait for the detective to arrive. It struck Garrett that a lot of people were worried about his control.

Matthias stood at the door to Lauren's office on the pier with some of his guys stationed outside, just in case. Garrett didn't see Matthias stepping in unless he lost all control, and Garrett had no intention of doing that.

Bob sat at the small table, flipping one of Lauren's pamphlets over in his hand, tapping one end then the other against the scarred wood in front of him. "What am I doing here?"

It was a fair question. Garrett had thought about bringing the police in and letting them handle it. That would have been the easier call, the smart one. But he wanted the satisfaction of seeing Bob's face when he got caught. "Admitting your guilt would be nice."

Bob's hand froze in midair. "What are you talking about?"

Garrett glanced at Matthias. He hadn't moved from his position at the door. Hadn't shown one ounce of emotion since they reviewed the evidence less than an hour ago and filled Lauren in.

"We set up video at Lauren's house." Garrett kept his fingers on the laptop keyboard facing him. "You're on it."

"I don't know—"

"Shut the fuck up and listen." Matthias stepped forward as he spoke. He stopped next to Bob, standing there. Looming over him and not doing anything to hide his frustration. It even vibrated on his voice.

"We know you were in on Carl's disappearance. You faked the financial documents to scam Lauren. You helped him fake his disappearance," Garrett said. When Bob leaned forward and his mouth dropped open, Garrett kept going. "No, I'm still talking."

Matthias leaned in even closer to Bob. "I'd listen to him."

"And then last night you broke into Lauren's house. Unfortunately for you, we were ready for you." Wren had cleaned up the video and sent it to Garrett this morning. Bob sneaking over the neighbor's fence and dropping into Lauren's yard. He went right to the cracked window as if he's been checking the place out since the murder.

"You don't know what you're talking about."

Matthias let out a long angry exhale as he looked at Garrett. "It's like he wants you to punch him."

"It does feel that way." Garrett spun the laptop around on the table for Bob to see the image frozen on it. "That's you, dumbass."

Bob was already shaking his head and shifting around in his chair. "You don't understand."

This should be good. "Explain it."

Funny how fast the tough-guy façade crumbled. Garrett had seen it a million times, across many cases, and it still fascinated him. Denial would turn to "how dare you" and defensive words, then panic set in. They babbled then.

Bob spread his hands on the table. He stared at them. Looked at the wall. Even glanced out the window. It took him what felt like forever to start talking again. "This was all Carl. He used me to trick Lauren."

So he was playing the role of victim. Interesting but not effective because Garrett did not buy it.

He leaned back in his chair and studied Bob. Maybe greed made the guy stupid. Garrett didn't know and didn't care so long as Lauren was safe. "Come up with a better story."

Matthias made a show of glancing at his watch. "And I'd do it fast because Detective Cryer is on his way to arrest you."

A screeching sound rang out in the room as Bob jumped up from his seat. The chair fell backward and he was on his feet. The darting eyes and crouched-to-run position made it clear he planned to play this the hard way.

The dumbass.

"Sit," Matthias ordered.

Garrett was not in the mood for extra drama. He pointed at the fallen chair. "Really, sit."

He wanted to fill Lauren in on events and then take her to dinner. After that they could spend the night, or a week or even more, in bed. He'd even celebrate the holiday if it meant being with her.

"You don't want to—" But it was too late. In the middle of Garrett's sentence Bob bolted. He made a run at the door and slammed into Matthias's chest instead. He hit Matthias hard enough that Garrett could hear a thud. "Did you really think that was going to work?"

Matthias grabbed Bob's suit jacket with one hand and picked up the chair with the other. He dropped the man into the seat without raising his voice. "I hope you're better with money than running, though the evidence you left behind suggests otherwise."

Garrett was done. He'd had enough nonsense and lying. It was time the men who committed the initial scam take responsibility. They'd flipped Lauren's life upside down. Now they could right it. Carl wasn't there, so the least they could do was wrap his investigation up, too.

For the first few minutes Bob stayed slumped in the chair. He stared at his hands and fiddled with his watch. Garrett was about to shove the table into his midsection when Bob finally spoke up. "I went to the house to get the documents."

The bank documents. It all came down to that initial scam. Garrett would bet Bob had carried out others since. He was trying to bury his tracks. But he'd gone too far and somewhere along the line fraud turned to murder. "This time. The last time you went and ran into Carl, and we know how that ended. Not great for Carl."

"No, you're wrong." Gone was the fidgeting and lack of eye contact. Bob faced Garrett head-on as he talked. "The money stuff, yes. Carl did it and didn't give me much of a choice but to help, but it stopped there."

"So you're only a certain type of criminal," Matthias said.

"I didn't kill Carl." Bob turned around in his chair. He looked from Matthias to Garrett. He pleaded with his voice and with his eyes. "I helped him before, that's true. Carl had these stories about Lauren and how terrible . . . But that's it."

Bob had convinced himself back then that Lauren deserved to get screwed. He didn't admit it, but Garrett could hear the excuses now. "You're trying to say you broke into Lauren's house once but not twice."

"I was looking for the bank statements. So long as Carl was supposedly dead there was no reason for Lauren to study them closely. She made it clear she needed the financial issues to be over. But with Carl being back, well, I thought Lauren might turn them in to the police this time and I couldn't let that happen." Bob made a strangled sound. "She's not under a microscope. Not like the last time, though I don't know why since the body was found in her house."

The guy had started spiraling and Garrett had heard enough. The detective could ferret it all out. "You aren't very convincing at pretending to be innocent."

The door bumped into Matthias's shoulder as it opened. A very pretty female face peeked inside. Garrett recognized her. The much younger, thoroughly involved Maryanne. Lauren might buy her story but Garrett couldn't separate out her part in the fraud from everything else.

She frowned as she looked around the room. "I'm sorry . . ."

Her entrance had Bob blinking and snapping out of his haze. "Maryanne?"

When she saw him, her eyes widened and her grip on the edge of the door tightened into a white-knuckle grip. "I'll come back."

"Stop." Matthias blocked her way, pushing her inside the room without ever touching her. That height did have its benefits.

Garrett tried to play good cop to Matthias's pushy cop. "What do you need?"

"Lauren." Maryanne's gaze flicked to Bob but did not linger.

"You told them." Anger shook Bob's voice.

Her knees seemed to give out as she reached for the closed door. "You know it was me?"

Matthias caught her before she hit the floor or anything else. "He does. We do."

Her vision seemed to come into focus as she looked at Garrett. "I remember you from that night. You were on the lawn with all the other police."

"We're investigating what happened to Carl." Garrett decided that wasn't exactly a lie.

"I left something out the other day." She inhaled. "Lauren was decent and I . . . I wanted her to know all of it."

Garrett had no idea what that meant. "Okay."

"Jake also knew. He was in on Carl's scam from the beginning." The words rushed out of her so fast that they slurred together.

It took an extra second for Garrett to separate them and understand what she was saying. "He helped his brother disappear and trick Lauren?"

"Carl thought it was funny," Bob said.

Maryanne nodded. "Carl knew Jake had a thing for Lauren. He used that to get him to play along. With Carl gone, Jake thought he had a chance with her."

"That's creepy as hell." Matthias shook his head. "I mean, come on."

Garrett had bigger worries. Matthias's people had been tracking all of the interested parties and there was one currently unaccounted for. "Where is Jake now?"

No one answered him.

LAUREN DIDN'T WANT any part of confronting Bob. He'd messed up so much of her life with his lies and deceit that it exhausted her to think about it. He set her up and then screwed her a second time by calling in those loans. It was a miracle he hadn't ruined her business for good.

That's why she was there, in the boat shed. With the paddles and boats hanging on the wall and the boat slip with the lapping water by her feet, it was one of her favorite places. She came here to think and to work. Waves caused water to splash against the slip and sometimes spill up and over the retaining wall until the enclosed space smelled like dead fish. For other people that might be a problem, not her.

She's thought she'd stored the artificial Christmas tree in there among all the other boxes and supplies. If so, she couldn't find it.

Giving up on the search, she opened one of the double doors and stepped into the cool December wind. The snow had passed north of them and socked in New York. They'd been lucky. At this time of year, they usually woke to a frozen ground and threats of snow and school closures. Instead, they had gray cloudy skies and a chill, but it was bearable.

She took one step and stopped suddenly. Her stomach sloshed around from the abruptness of it. Seeing Jake standing there, uncharacteristically disheveled and shaking his head, threw her off. She hadn't expected him and he hated boats, so he rarely ventured out past the marina to this more secluded, nontouristy spot.

"What are you doing here?" When he stood there with wild eyes and stiff shoulders, not talking, she tried again. "Jake?"

"Some business guy from DC?"

The words sounded clear but they didn't make any sense. She knew he was grieving, but this was so out of the ordinary that she started to worry he had some sort of health issue.

She reached out and put her hand on his forearm. "What are you talking about?"

He glanced down at her fingers. "I've given you time. Room. Then I heard about this other guy, but I convinced myself he was a client."

She dropped her hand as her heart began to race. "You're talking about Garrett?"

"Carl said you were cold, but I never believed him. See, I saw you first. I talked about asking you out then he came in and . . ." Jake shook his head. "It doesn't matter now."

Lauren backed up until her shoes hit the door. "Maybe we should—"

"He promised he wasn't coming back." Jake stopped scanning the area and stared at her then. Fury filled his intense gaze. "That you were mine."

Her stomach heaved. She had to force her body to remain still as she swallowed. "I'm not yours, Jake. You know that. What are you saying?"

"He ran through all the money and Maryanne got needy. He hated needy women."

He was talking about some of the people who'd made her life hell. Jake mentioned them as if he'd sat around the table and planned it all with them. Then it hit her . . . he had. She'd been blaming Bob, and that made sense. But Jake was a part of this, too. He was the person Carl ran to when he got back to town. He's the one Carl would have bragged to about Maryanne back then.

Her heartbeat thundered in her ears and her legs shook so hard she was surprised she could still stand. She fought it all back, the waves of panic and the numbing fear, and stayed focused.

She thought about her phone and tried to remember where she'd put it. She could scream but between the wind and her distance from the marina and office, no one would ever hear her. That left fighting and running, and she was prepared to do both.

First, she tried to calm him. "Jake. Let's go to the diner and talk about this."

"So you can run to your new boyfriend? That's not going to happen."

The comment made sense. No matter what was happening in his head, he wasn't too far gone. Reason didn't work but more drastic means might. "What do you think is going to happen between us?"

"You need to fix this."

She nudged the door open behind her. If she could slip inside then she could grab a weapon. She calculated the chances of that choice versus just bolting. In his mood, she had no idea what Jake would do or if he had any weapons on him. She couldn't see any, but his thick jacket could hide a lot of scary things.

"*I killed Carl for you.*" He delivered the rage-filled words through clenched teeth.

They punched into her brain and sat there. She felt dizzy and sick. The need to throw up almost overtook her this time. "Jake, please."

"He was going to step in and ruin your life again. I tried to talk him out of it but he just laughed."

"What did you do?"

"Carl had to leave. The documents, the money . . . I know it hurt for a while. But you rebuilt everything. You made the business more successful than it ever was." A smile broke across his face. "I was so proud of how hard you worked. I couldn't let Carl come in and rip it apart."

She preferred his yelling. The smile scared the hell out of her. "You were at my house?"

"I followed him there." He sounded so logical now.

The words came out clear, as if he were explaining a simple math problem and not a horrific crime. "He planned to be there when you got home, force the issue."

She wedged her heel in the opening of the door and kept it there. "So, you killed him."

"It was a fight, Lauren. You get that, right? An accident." Jake shook his head. "He wouldn't stop. You know how this sort of thing happens."

The familiar tone convinced her to move. She kicked the door open and ducked inside, only to panic when she couldn't make her fingers work fast enough to find the lock and use it. Adrenaline surged through her as her hands fumbled on the metal lock and her gaze scanned the low-lit area in a frantic search for her phone. She didn't see it, but she almost had the lock.

Without warning the door slammed into her, pushing her back. She turned to see Jake standing there. He didn't have a frying pan this time. He carried a knife and wore a blank expression, a sort of resignation to what he had to do next.

She put up her hands, knowing she couldn't fend off a blade. "It's okay."

"You still don't get it." He pointed the tip of the knife at her then at his own chest. "We make sense together. We have more in common than you ever did with Carl. He took you for granted but I wouldn't. I have been waiting for you. Been patient."

All of the blood drained from her head. She fought to stay coherent. "Absolutely."

"Don't patronize me, Lauren. I'm not deranged or evil. This—us—we just make sense. My idiot brother didn't get it. He schemed and planned and tricked and that got him things, but only for a short time. You deserved more."

The keys. His familiarity with her house from having been in it so many times. The way she welcomed him into her office and her life. And all along he'd been planning.

When he took a step toward her, she moved. A scream tore from her throat as she lunged to the side, grabbing for the wall. Her hands slammed against tools and a paddle, sending the equipment falling and making it rattle. Her fingers blindly searched as she backed up and watched him. So many things happening at once.

Her hand closed over the end of a paddle. She ripped it from the wall, knowing she would only have one shot at this. Refusing to hesitate, she acted. Her battle cry rang out as she yanked the makeshift weapon off the hooks. Put all her energy and strength behind it and swung.

The paddle skimmed the air. A smooth motion sent it sailing. She held on, bellowing her enraged scream and not letting go as the paddle end slammed into his shoulder, right by his neck. It was like running headfirst into a wall. The force shook her entire body.

She closed her eyes for a second, so brief. She opened them in time to see Jake drop to his knees. He listed to one side but he didn't go down. The knife waved in his hand, through the air.

Her muscles froze. She watched the blood soak through his jacket. Saw him struggle to stand up.

"Jake, no," she begged as she tried to tighten her hands on the paddle again, but her fingers refused to move.

The room whirled around and her vision started to blur. She hadn't been hurt but her body was giving in. The adrenaline high burned out.

He had one foot on the ground and started to rise as a voice shouted in her head to move. She tried to get past him to the door but he fell against her. A hand latched on to her leg with a surprisingly strong grip. She kicked and yelled and tried to fling her body to the side.

Just as she lifted the paddle again, hoping to gather the strength from somewhere deep inside her, the door slammed open. Garrett and Matthias rushed to fill the space.

Garrett took the first step. He rammed his foot into Jake's arm, sending the knife flying. The second shot nailed Jake in the back. He dropped in an unmoving sprawl.

Men poured into the room then. Ones she remembered from her house, Matthias's men. Then the detective. She couldn't figure out where they came from or what was happening. Her mind refused to focus and her brain kept misfiring.

Her body started to drop and Garrett was right there. He slid across the floor on his knees and caught her. Wrapped his strong arms around her. "I've got you."

He did. He was there and protecting her. Not running away. "Garrett?"

The room exploded into activity around them. Jake's eyes were closed and Matthias had him pinned down. She watched as the detective put handcuffs on him.

"Lauren, are you okay?" Concern sounded in Garrett's voice.

She could only think about one thing. "I knew you'd come."

Chapter Eleven

GARRETT HAD STAYED in Annapolis longer than planned. Christmas was coming up fast, only four days away now. His worst time of the year. The time he generally could not hang out with people. But this year he wanted to. The idea of leaving Lauren . . . yeah, he couldn't even think about that. Not when waking up with her each morning had become his favorite thing.

She'd sat across from him last night at the dinner table and talked over burgers about going out to buy a fresh tree. Something about lights and how one bulb always burned out. One she couldn't find and it ruined the whole strand. His mind had stopped working as her eyes lit up and she debated the right size tree to fit her room.

The tree talk led to Christmas dinner talk. The discussion sounded familiar. Lotti and his aunt used all sorts of arguments to lure him home each year. The promise of the perfect gravy was a favorite.

But this was Lauren. Practical Lauren. She'd never been a big talker, but the stress had lifted. Jake and Bob were the police's problem now. Both were looking at jail time; for Jake, it would be a lot.

Lauren being Lauren, she talked the detective and the prosecutor and anyone who would listen out of pursuing charges against Maryanne. She'd helped at the end, Lauren insisted. Garrett guessed Lauren's choice was more about knowing what it was like to live with Carl than wanting to give the younger woman a break. Either way, the move made him smile.

Everything she did made him smile. He loved her tenacity and calm. She plowed through problems and refused to view herself as a victim. Her loyalty to Kayla and the way she joked with Matthias—it all worked for Garrett. It also scared him shitless.

He glanced at his cell and finished the text conversation with Lotti. The one he'd started right after a brief check-in with his aunt. It sounded to him like Lotti had found an interesting way to spend the holiday and was trying to hide it. The idea made him laugh. It also made it easier for him not to jump on a plane and go keep her company.

You didn't get to Cabo.

Lotti wrote back in less than five seconds. Mom's such a tattletale. Weather's bad.

She didn't say anything about the weather. She had hopes you were with a guy. So did Garrett. He loved Lotti and wanted her to be happy . . . then he could tease her until she begged for mercy.

Is there a point to this conversation?

That sounded like defense mode to Garrett. Just remember, if his name starts with a letter between A and Z, he's likely to ruin your life. You were warned.

He decided to sign off before she shot something back at him. With that done, he could concentrate on Lauren and watch as she unpacked a box of ornaments. The homemade lopsided ones and shiny red balls. The box housed a treasure trove of collected items from years past.

She turned around with an odd look on her face. A smile, but it seemed fake. Like she was forcing it. "Did you want to help me decorate the tree before you go? If so, we need to go find one."

Before you go . . . "Am I leaving?"

"You said you weren't a holiday guy. And I thought . . ." Her already dim smile vanished. "We got caught up in everything that was happening here. The danger and Carl. The not knowing."

"What are you saying?" Because he didn't have a clue.

"I texted you about Carl and didn't really give you a choice *not* to be involved. Now you can get back to your plans."

The world flipped on him. The walls between them had come down over the last week. He'd chipped away at her impressive defenses and negotiated his way around them until they really were dating. And now this.

The reality that she was turning them off, sending him away—again—and acting as if they were friends but little more than that hit him like a body blow. He felt the shot straight to his chest and it nearly doubled him over.

He stood up and walked around to the back of the couch. Put the furniture between them and tried not to notice when she flinched. "You're kicking me out."

"I'm telling you not to feel obligated." She swallowed hard enough for him to see it across the room. "The tree means something to me, but the rest of the holiday doesn't. You don't need to stick around when I know you'd rather be by yourself."

This was bullshit. Complete bullshit. The only question was if she really said all this for him or if this was about her hiding in plain sight again.

Matthias and Kayla had invited her to spend the day with all of them. They'd get her through the rough day while the brother-in-law she thought she knew spent the holiday in a cell. But that didn't mean she wanted to spend it with him, and now that he realized that he could barely think. "Is this some sort of fear of commitment thing?"

Her hands shook as she put the ornament down on the coffee table. "It's for you. I saw your bag when I got out of the shower an hour ago. It's packed. You've been on the phone with your cousin in California. I can read the signs."

Her response set his head on fire. Instead of talking to him, she was back to assessing and analyzing and guessing and not talking. "If you have a question for me, Lauren, ask it."

"I've got to tell you I didn't see that part coming. Not from the guy who begged for a date for months." Her head fell to the side. "Or are you *that* guy? The one who likes the chase but nothing else."

"You've got this all wrong."

Her hands dropped to her lap. "Then explain it to me."

"My parents died on Christmas Eve." He shared the unshareable because saying anything else would not be enough. "I don't celebrate. And, yeah, you're right. I usually run but that wasn't the plan today." Even as her expression softened and her mouth dropped open, he continued to reel. The idea that it would always be this way with her, with her hiding her feelings and pushing him away, had his temper spiking.

She came over to him then. "I'm so sorry, but . . ."

"What?" He barked out the question.

She retreated then. Pulled back and kept that safe distance between them. "You have a life. I have a life."

"You have got to be shitting me." Not his most eloquent line, but the words tumbled out of him and he didn't bother to pretty them up because he didn't feel pretty right now.

His attraction to her nearly snapped him in half. He kept looking for things he didn't like and nothing came to him except what was happening this minute. She wasn't perfect but he loved that, too.

Loved. That was the problem. He made sure he loved only few people. He kept that circle tight and she blew it wide open.

"I lost a husband and my family. I had to rebuild everything." Her voice started out soft then got louder. "Is it that weird that I need some time to figure out who and what I want?"

From anyone else, maybe not. From her it felt like one more excuse.

Matthias had warned him. Garrett ignored the alarm because he'd thought they had gotten past the part where she pushed him away and made him prove himself by running back. They'd slept together, woken up together, survived Jake together. She'd trusted him and leaned on him and now she was stepping back. Shoving him away and making him work for it.

He was so fucking tired of this. She shredded him with this lack of trust.

Here he'd thought he would be the one running today. True, he did pack the bag. Out of habit. Out of years of pain over the holiday. He'd planned to explain all of that to her, but that was before she gave him the it's-time-to-go speech. If this went on much longer she might hit him with the it's-not-you-it's-me line and then he would really lose it.

"I fell for you, Lauren." His words floated there in the room, amid the half-unwrapped ornaments and the cleared space where the tree might go. He'd meant to hold them back, but what the hell did he have to lose now? "Do you get that?"

"It's only been a short time and—"

"Fucking stop with that." He shook his head until he thought he'd get sick from it. "We've been doing this dance for months. Stop pretending what's happening between us is new."

"Don't you dare talk to me like that." She walked over to the chair by the door and picked up his coat. "No man is going to yell at me again and not get it thrown back at him."

He saw it then. The fear and pain in her eyes. The way she held her body frozen, still. She was mistaking him for Carl, and he hated that, but he needed to give her a breath to fix that thought. "Look, Lauren . . ."

"I'm done with men treating me like I don't get to make choices."

The words dunked him right back into a pool of fury. She refused to separate him from Carl and it pissed him off. "I am not your idiot former husband."

But her expression suggested she'd made up her

mind and had no room for him to try to maneuver her. She shoved the coat into his chest. "Get. Out."

TWO DAYS LATER Lauren stood in the Christmas tree lot and looked at the slim choices left over. Most were too big. She'd have to cut a hole in her roof to fit them in. Others looked a little sickly. Truth was, she didn't care about any of them. Losing Garrett had sucked the life right out of Christmas for her.

Watching him leave ripped her apart. She hadn't been able to eat or sleep since. Her breath still came in harsh gasps if she let her mind wander back to their limited days together.

But that was the point. They were officially dating for a short time, but they had been around each other, connected to each other, for so much longer. Months of getting to know each other. Him breaking down her defenses. And now she was alone.

The crappy part was that it had been her decision. She'd shoved him out the door. All that talk about his parents and hating the holiday . . . it had shaken her. She'd tried to push him away before he could leave and she'd done a hell of a job.

Her first call this morning was to Matthias to get information on where Garrett might be, but Matthias was out. How convenient.

Her next move was to swallow her pride and text

Garrett. She'd typed the words then deleted then typed again. Hitting Send took all of her strength. She had to block out her memories of the past and her doubts about the future and do the one thing she'd long stopped doing—hope.

Call me. That's all she wrote because the rest of the words needed to be delivered in person. She owed him an apology. She needed to see his face as she explained how her walls inched up without any signal from her brain. How she shut down when he raised her voice, even though she knew he had every right.

She'd sent the text sixty-eight minutes ago and nothing.

A dragging mix of frustration and sadness swamped her at the lack of response. He always texted back immediately and she'd had no idea how much she counted on that until right now.

The temptation to go home and curl up on her couch hit her, but she fought it off. She needed something happy and she refused to go through the holiday without a tree. It was a matter of principle. It was her house. Her holiday. She would make it happen then turn a corner in her life. Finally move forward . . . somehow.

She stopped in front of a four-foot tree. It managed to be both too short and too tall. Flurries whirled around her head. None of it stuck to the ground but a few specks melted in her hair.

"You should wear a hat."

He was there. At the sound of Garrett's voice, she

spun around so fast she slipped on a slick spot in the grass. Her heart thudded loud enough to drown out everything else. She tried to think of the right thing to say but nothing came to her.

Her gaze wandered over him. She took in the tired eyes and thin line of his mouth. She could see black pants and a jacket and little else because he'd bundled up tight in his jacket and scarf.

"You're here." It was the first thing that popped into her brain.

He glanced around, his gaze lingering on the trees. That's all it took for her sympathy to rise. With everything that had passed between them, she knew it had to be hard for him here.

He kept coming back and one of these times he wouldn't. The thought made her want to heave.

When his gaze shot back to her some of the cloudiness had cleared. "I'm here for you. Because I can't stay away."

It would be so unfair to give her hope then snatch it away. That wasn't who he was or had ever been with her, but trust came hard for her. She'd been tested and bruised, but when it came to him her armor fell.

"You were so angry," she said, trying to block out his face when he walked out the door.

"Because it felt like you gave up on us. That you wanted to push us back into what we were." He shook his head. "I'll negotiate and fight, but I can't just be your friend, Lauren."

"I don't want that." She abandoned thoughts about trees and the holidays and concentrated on him. Said the words that made her ache. "I missed you."

He closed his eyes for a second. When he opened them again some of the exhaustion had cleared. "Two damn days and I missed you so much I couldn't see straight."

The breath rushed out of her so quickly her chest burned. "I've been so careful for so long."

"Me, too." He slipped off his gloves and stuffed them in his pockets. "But I don't want to be. Not anymore."

The words chipped away at the wall she'd built to hold him back. They sounded so familiar because that's how she lived, too. "What changed?"

"I met this hot woman with a boat and she turned my life upside down." He put his hands on her hips. "I screwed up and yelled. I walked out when I should have stayed and fought."

"I pushed you."

His smile didn't reach his eyes but his hands were soothing. They skimmed up and down her arms, pulling her closer. "I negotiate for a living. I convince people to do things, but I couldn't think of a way to make you understand that for the first time ever, I don't want to be alone in December."

He said the right things. Snagged her with this intense look that held her in that spot. "I've spent my whole life pushing people away but I can't watch you leave me again."

That's not what she meant to say. But then he was in front of her, holding her. She wanted to wipe the pain off his face and take him home with her. Forget her past and her relationship failures. Put Carl and the pain of being lied to aside and focus on the man who had been nothing but decent and devoted for months. The one she took for granted.

"I was hoping you'd let me help you with the tree." His voice actually cracked as he spoke.

A rush of love swamped her. "That sounds like something people who are dating and committed might do."

"I want both of those things with you." He dropped a soft kiss on her nose. "I at least want us to try. Tell me what you want and I'll try to give it to you."

"You're negotiating." And she loved it because he didn't just expect her to change and give in. For him it was a back and forth.

His hand cupped her cheek. "This is the most important negotiation of my life."

Everything she never knew she wanted loomed in front of her. All she had to do was reach out and grab it. Take the risk.

She slipped her hand over his. "I'm not easy."

He snorted. "I've got you beat. I've spent years running away from ornaments and Christmas carols. I've blocked the whole holiday."

Laughter bubbled up inside her. "You understand that I'm halfway down the road to loving you. I think it started months ago, but it happened."

She stood there and waited. Weeks ago she would have accepted less. She'd had no expectation of caring about anyone. But now she knew him and believed, truly believed, that they could build something. They had baggage and walls to break down, but she was betting that he was worth it. That he wouldn't care about the stupid stuff or comment on the size of her thighs. He would never steal from her.

But it would be better if he moved or spoke or did *anything*. "Garrett?"

"I never wanted holidays and a future before you. You give me everything." He wrapped his arms around her and pulled her close. "I couldn't go two days without you. Give me a chance to prove it to you."

He whispered the words against her mouth before he kissed her. His mouth slid over hers in a kiss that started out frantic then morphed into something sexy and inviting. A promise of what they could have if they worked at it.

After a minute, he lifted his head and looked down at her. "When you get the rest of the way down that road to loving me, I'll be waiting there for you." He finally smiled. "You're stuck with me, Lauren. I'm pretty sure I've proven that."

She'd never heard anything better. Not a full declaration, not for either of them. But a place to start. Something to build. She didn't fight it. "We need a tree."

His eyes didn't fill with fear this time when he looked

around the lot. "You pick. I already have what I need to get through the holiday."

"Sweet-talker."

He winked at her. "Wait till you see my expertise with a string of lights."

The joking, his smiles. She didn't really need anything else. "Actually, I'm in charge of decorating. Like, forever."

"We'll negotiate the details." His mouth brushed over hers.

She loved the thought of that, of arguing and joking with him over silly things. "You are a great negotiator."

He laughed. "That's what I've been saying."

"Then let's get that tree and go home and do some negotiating."

"Yeah, you're definitely perfect for me." He dropped another kiss on her mouth. Quick and sweet. "No doubt about it."

Keep reading for a sneak peek at the third book in
HelenKay Dimon's Games People Play series,

THE PRETENDER

They say it takes a thief to catch a thief, and Harrison
Tate is proof. Once a professional burglar, he now makes
a lawful living tracking down stolen art. No one needs
to know about his secret sideline, "liberating" artifacts
acquired through underhanded methods. At least until
one of those jobs sees him walking in on a murder.

Gabrielle Wright has long been estranged from
her wealthy family, but she didn't kill her sister.
Trouble is, the only person who can prove it is the
sexy, elusive criminal who shouldn't have been at
the island estate on that terrible night. She's not
expecting honor among thieves—or for their mutual
attraction to spark into an intense inferno of desire.

Under the guise of evaluating her family's art, Harris
comes back to the estate hoping to clear Gabby's name.
But returning to the scene of the crime has never
been riskier, with their hearts and lives on the line.

Chapter One

HARRISON TATE DIDN'T believe in luck. He believed in planning. Right now, he needed the luck.

He blinked a few times, hoping the scene in front of him would change. No body, no blood . . . nope, it was all still there.

A woman—*the* woman—the one who stuck to a schedule and rarely ventured outside a three-mile area. She should have been reading at the dock, as she did every nonrainy day at this time for the last three weeks. Sitting there, watching the waves lap up on the stone retaining wall that separated the Chesapeake Bay from Tabitha Island. Her private island.

He'd staked out the isolated land, this house and this woman for more than a month. Watched from a boat at one point and from the small uninhabited island a short distance away at another. He'd been able to hack into the camera on her laptop. He knew when she was working on it, which was almost always.

He'd tracked her movements, knew her schedule. But on the ride over here he'd missed seeing someone else go into her house. Someone who wanted more from her than a painting.

The longer he stood there, looming over her still body, the more he became locked in a confining shell he could not break. Less than thirty seconds had passed since he walked into the old-school library with its dark floor-to-ceiling bookshelves and massive desk positioned in front of the French doors to the small patio outside. He'd found her there, sprawled on the floor with her eyes closed and her chest not moving. Blood pooled around her and seeped into the muted gray carpet beneath her.

Just as his brain signaled to his hand to grab his cell and call for help, her eyes popped open. Stunning green. That fact registered in his mind. Next came her fear. It bounced off the walls and pummeled him. Her body shook with it.

She reached out and her fingertips brushed his pants right near his calf. She likely thought she grabbed him and pulled hard, but he barely felt the touch. Whatever energy she possessed had been spent during the furious battle that waged in the room before he got there. Glass shattered on the floor, an overturned table. Books and papers scattered everywhere.

He dropped down, balancing on the balls of his feet,

and reached for her hand. He still wore his gloves but she didn't seem to notice. She kept mouthing something. A soundless word he couldn't make out. He leaned in with his ear right over her mouth, trying to pick up a thread or any noise but that didn't work either.

He pulled back and looked into her eyes. They were clouded now and unfocused. "Tabitha?"

He knew her name because he made it his business to know the people from whom he planned to liberate any number of items. In her case, a specific painting that usually hung over the fireplace in this room. It balanced there now, ripped from the wall with one edge hanging over the mantel. Teetering, ready to fall. All eleven million dollars of it.

"Help me." The words came out of her on a strangled cry. Her chest heaved as she fought for breath.

He could see her wince as she inhaled. Her hand slipped out of his as all the tension drained out of her. Her eyes rolled back then closed.

"No, no, no." This time he started mouth-to-mouth. He blew and counted, trying to remember the precise sequence from every television show where he'd seen it performed and from a class he'd taken more than a decade ago.

Nothing worked.

He moved, thinking to press down on her chest, but the wound was right there. A slashing cut that left a gaping seam close to her sternum. Another slice into her abdomen. There was no question her attacker had unleashed a wild frenzy on her. Someone wanted her dead. He didn't, but he had no idea where to push to save her or how to get her heart beating again either.

A crackling energy raced through him right behind an uncharacteristic panic. He prided himself on his ability to stay calm and handle nearly anything. He'd been trained to maneuver through any situation. Use charm, strength or pure nerve to battle his way out. Right now, every cell was alive and on fire and desperate to do something.

He clamped down on his fight-or-flight instincts and reached for the burner cell tucked in his back pocket. He had no idea how long it would take for reinforcements to arrive, but he'd stay as long as possible. Try to keep her breathing but leave enough lead time to escape.

One thing was true. He could not be caught here . . . or anywhere.

He'd just hit the first button to make the call as he heard the sound. A gurgling in her throat, as if she was drowning in her own body. An openmouthed labored breath . . . then a shocking stillness. Saliva dribbled out of the corner of her mouth as her head dropped to one side.

The death rattle. Had to be. He'd never heard it before and never wanted to hear it again.

He slid off his gloves and checked for a pulse. Nothing. She was gone.

With his brain in freefall, he lost his balance and tipped forward. Landed hard on his knees as every part of him shut down. For a few seconds he couldn't think. Couldn't get a single muscle to move. He stared at her, willing her to jump up or reach for him again. Anything.

The stillness in the room mirrored her unmoving body. He now knew silence could thump and beat just like a sound. The second later reality pounded him. Smells came rushing back to him. An unexpected scent he couldn't place.

A door thudded. He pegged it as a screen, which likely meant the front door.

"Tabitha?" A woman's voice floated through the oversized rooms. "I thought we were going to meet at the dock twenty minutes ago."

The sister.

She'd been a surprise. Intriguing . . . a mystery. People whispered about her. They jumped to conclusions based on rumors. He had and now regretted it. Under different circumstances he'd take the time to meet her and see how deep her secrets ran.

All the stories about the sisters' estrangement turned out to be untrue. All the talk about her being disowned. None of that mattered now because she was there, in the house. She was about to stumble into a horror and Harris couldn't protect her from it. She'd be plunged into a hell worse than his.

He scrambled to his feet. Right as he turned to run back through the doors to the outside a thought hit him. His mind rebelled at the thought of what he needed to do. The pure sickness of it. His gaze zipped to the doorway before he bent down and used his glove to wipe Tabitha's mouth. To erase any signs that he'd tried to save her.

When he stood back up a sensation hit him. Self-loathing. Maybe he was a fucking asshole just as his father claimed.

Footsteps sounded on the hardwood in the hallway. "Tabitha? Enough with the online sleuthing for today. It's beautiful outside."

Harris couldn't wait another second. In a soundless jog, he stepped around the body. He'd already kneeled and walked through the scene, likely made it impossible for a forensic team to discover anything of value. His only goal now was not to track blood in a path directly to him.

The handle slipped in his hand, but he finally got the door open. He'd made it outside and into the sunshine when he heard the sister's voice again.

"Hey, who are—"

He didn't stop or look around. Didn't wait to explain or comfort her. He pulled off his shoes and his feet hit the grass. He started running.

And then the screaming started. A high-pitched wailing that tore through him. A mix of shock and pain so raw it ripped away his defenses and slammed his body to a halt. Right there on the perfect lawn with the blue water shining all around the island, he froze. Not for long, but long enough to hear the sister's gulping cries.

He shook his head and took off again. Ignoring the boat dock and the small beach there, he ran in the opposite direction to the rocky shoreline. To his small boat. He climbed over a rock ledge and down to the water's edge.

Waves crashed in a soothing beat that clashed with the images rewinding in his mind. They would haunt him. All of this would. Tabitha. Her sister. The blood.

He skipped the boat and went right for the water. Nothing in the stolen craft would trace back to him. He'd worn gloves the entire time, so no fingerprints to be found. As he plunged into the water, splashes of red mixed with the blue. He looked down and realized blood coated his pants. Now it mixed with the Bay and slipped farther away from him with each new wave.

Trying to call up every ounce of training, he mentally walked through his steps into the main house. It took only seconds but felt like a full-length movie unspooled in his brain. Satisfied he'd covered his tracks, he turned the boat over and pushed it down until water bubbled up inside. He didn't need to sink it, just be sure any unexpected traces and fibers disappeared.

He heard yelling. A man's voice. It grew more faint as Harris saw a figure running for the front porch of the house from the far edge of the island. Away from Harris, not toward him. Likely the island caretaker responding to the sister's screams.

That was all the incentive Harris needed. People were moving. Law enforcement would appear. The press—

everyone. The Wright family had money. Stupid money. They would not stop until they caught the killer, and he refused to be tagged as that.

He needed to swim. To get to the smaller island nearby. From there he could call his reinforcements.

The way he got to the main island, by rowing, was too dangerous now. People would remember everything they saw the day Tabitha Wright was stabbed to death. A man rowing at breakneck speed dressed all in black and wearing gloves would stick out. No, he had to bide his time. Hide among the overgrown trees on the island two hundred feet away and let the people he trusted figure out how to extract him.

But he had to get there first, so he started swimming. A few strokes then he dove under. The tide crashed on him, stealing his breath. He didn't care. This was life or death. First, hers. Now his.

Even being in good shape and with the protection of the narrow strait between the two islands minimizing the waves, the tide spun him around. For every two strokes, he seemed to fall back one. He forced his mind to focus and his body to pump even harder. Water filled his mouth, not as salty as the ocean but the taste lingered. His ears clogged. The advance took an eternity and his lungs burned from the effort.

Just as his arms gave out, his knee brushed against the rocky coast of the smaller island. A thwapping sounded above him. He recognized it. Helicopters.

Keeping low, he crawled up into the brush. A jagged edge shredded his pants and slit his skin but he barely felt the cut. The sound of his heavy breathing echoed around him. Branches and some plant with sharp needles jabbed into him, but he kept going.

He shimmied on his knees and elbows until he landed in the protected cover of the overhanging trees. Turning over, he stared up into the canopy of green. Patches of blue sky poked through the trees and fluffy white clouds blew by.

On any other day, under any other circumstances he would declare it a perfect day to be outside. But today was his nightmare. A job gone deadly wrong.

He closed his eyes and the haunting sound of the sister's cries came rushing back to him. He feared the noise would always fill his brain, as would the guilt of not being able to do enough for Tabitha, a woman he didn't actually know.

Exhaustion tugged at him. He could feel his muscles crying out for rest. For a bed. For quiet. For any place that was not here.

He turned onto his side and forced his body up on one elbow. His joints groaned in protest. At thirty-four that never happened, but he didn't have any energy left. The adrenaline surge that got him across that water had all but vanished. Now he lay there in the shade, wet and with cooling skin.

He pushed up to his knee and his body buckled. He

couldn't put any weight on his left side. Even through the dark, soaked clothes he saw a fresh spurt of blood. It stained the ground where he'd just kneeled. He used his gloved palm to cover the red blotch with dirt.

Pushing the whole way up, he hobbled on one leg. Half bounced and half dragged his body over to the nearest tree trunk and tried to get his bearings. He'd staked out Tabitha Island from here and left backup supplies. His Plan B. Random items without any identifying marks. The most important being a satellite phone. The ultimate emergency safeguard that he had planned to double back and pick up when he finished the job.

So much for thinking today's work would be fast and easy.

It took another five minutes to get to his hiding place. A helicopter had landed on the island and boats were circling, some filled with tourists looking to see what was happening and others in transit to likely lock the place down.

He reached for the duffle bag and ripped the zipper open. He still wore the gloves. They were molded to his hands now and stiff. He dialed one of the few numbers he ever called. If the sat phone was the backup plan, this phone number qualified as the end-of-the-world measure he never wanted to invoke.

The line rang once then a deep voice came on the line. "Yes?"

That was it. No greeting or introduction. Just a stern, half-angry bark. For the first time in an hour Harris felt relief. Like he might actually survive today.

"It's Harris." He blew out a long breath and said the words he'd vowed *never* to say again. "I need you."

About the Author

HELENKAY DIMON spent the years before becoming a romance author as a divorce attorney. Not the usual transition, she knows. Good news is she now writes full-time and is much happier. She has sold over forty novels and novellas to numerous publishers. Her nationally bestselling and award-winning books have been showcased in numerous venues and her books have twice been named Red-Hot Reads and excerpted in *Cosmopolitan* magazine. You can learn more at her website: www.helenkaydimon.com.

Discover great authors, exclusive offers and more at hc.com.

A Letter from the Editor

Dear Reader,

I hope you liked the latest romance from Avon Impulse! If you're looking for another steamy, fun, emotional read, be sure to check out some of our upcoming titles. Historical romance fans are in luck because we have two great new titles this winter!

First up, we have another male/male romance from Cat Sebastian coming in December! IT TAKES TWO TO TUMBLE launches Cat's brand new series, Seducing the Sedgwicks, and it's a steamy story of a country vicar who is asked to help wrangle the children of a stern but gloriously handsome sea captain . . . the two men can't seem to keep their hands off each other!

In January, we have a delightful, charming debut novel from Marie Tremayne! LADY IN WAITING features a runaway bride who takes a position as a maid in a lord's household. He's incredibly tempted by his new servant but he knows they can never be together due to class differences . . . or can they? You don't want to miss this fantastic first book in Marie's *Reluctant Brides* trilogy!

You can purchase any of these titles by clicking the links above or by visiting our website, www. AvonRomance.com. Thank you for loving romance as much as we do . . . enjoy!

Sincerely,
Nicole Fischer
Editorial Director
Avon Impulse